Pizza To Die For

Lea Wait

USA Today best-selling author

Sheepscot River Press

ISBN 978-0-9964084-5-5

DEDICATION

For my children, Caroline, Ali, Becky and Elizabeth, who survived growing up in the suburbs of New Jersey.

And for my grandchildren, Victoria, Vanessa, Taylor, Samantha, Drew, AJ, Henry and Maddy, all of whom are hidden in this book. (Can you find them?) A special thank you to Vanessa and Samantha for testing Mikki's recipes … and to my husband, Bob Thomas, for eating the results.

Chapter 1

I'm Mikki Norden, I'm fourteen, and my life is already ruined.

Six weeks ago my dad left Mom and me. He's now living with my best friend's mom, and, of course, with my best friend.

I never want to see her or Dad again, and I probably won't, because after Mom stopped crying she announced, "Pack all your things. Now. We're flying to New Jersey to stay with your Gramma Rosa."

A grandmother I'd never met.

I didn't even have time to say goodbye to friends I'd had since kindergarten.

Mom threw out both our cellphones. She said we didn't need anyone in Seattle. We were starting over. "Leaving the scene of the crime," is actually how she put it.

So now I'm going to Edgewood High School, the same school Mom went to centuries ago, where the kids dress like they're models in store catalogs, and no one's heard of the Seattle Seahawks.

Most of the time Mom stays in the bedroom she had when she was my age, and plans murders.

Wait! Don't dial 911! Mom's a mystery writer. At our house poisons and alibis have always been part of normal dinner conversation. Dad was really good at suggesting clues and plot twists.

We didn't know he was also plotting an end to our family.

And speaking of mysteries ... something strange is going on here in Edgewood. If I tell anyone Gramma Rosa's last name (it's D'Andrea) they act like they've just smelled garbage.

When I asked Mom, "Why?" she looked up from her laptop long enough to say, "Ignore them. Just tell people your name is Miki Norden and you're from Seattle. Don't mention your grandparents." Well, it's not as if I go around talking about my grandparents. But everyone in town seems to know who they are anyway, and for some reason hardly anyone speaks to me.

On top of everything, even though I hate him for ruining our lives, I really miss Dad. I know that doesn't make sense. And I don't tell Mom, because she'll just say, "Cope, Mikki." Which is Mom-talk for "suck it up." It's not easy for her, either. Some nights I hear her crying.

A couple of years ago I got really sick. Dad was so worried he stayed home from work for a couple of days to take care of me. He brought me a stuffed Cheshire Cat, and read *Alice in Wonderland* out loud, even though I was old enough to read it myself. I loved the way he acted out the Mock Turtle and the March Hare. That time, me in bed and Dad reading to me, is one of my favorite memories. Despite everything, I brought Cat with me from Seattle. Now she's on my new bed.

Right now I feel like Alice. I've fallen down a rabbit hole and ended up in a place where I don't fit, and nothing makes sense.

Dad's probably reading *Alice in Wonderland* to Sung Ja.

I want to think Dad misses us. Or at least misses me. I've secretly emailed him, when I could get my hands on Mom's computer, and twice I tried calling him on Gramma Rose's telephone.

He e-mailed me back. Once. "Mikki, it's not my fault. Your mother took you to New Jersey. Talk to her about it. Love, Dad."

So who can I talk to? The only people who understand me are Gramma Rosa and Mr. Baldacci. They're both old and Italian. Gramma Rosa's seventy-sixth birthday is Friday. She uses a sparkly pink wheeling walker and she gets wobbly after she has a little too much afternoon Chianti, an Italian wine she says makes her joints feel better.

Her friend Mr. Baldacci (he says I can call him "Mr. B") is an awesome chef. He owns Baldacci's, an Italian restaurant just down the hill, and he's the one who told me what Chianti was. He's told me a lot of other things about Italy and Italian food, too.

They're things I need to know. First, because I'm half Italian (Mom) as well as half Norwegian (Dad). (Add that to the list of things Mom never told me.) And, second, because I'm going to be a great chef someday, and everyone loves Italian food. I've watched cooking shows on TV for years, and I have a bookcase full of cookbooks that I study every night before I go to bed.

Everyone likes to eat good food. So when I'm a chef I won't always have to look for a new job, like Dad does, or write books that no one will publish, like Mom. Who rejects German chocolate cake?

Mr. B says he's really impressed with my culinary talents.

He's the very first chef I've known personally. He's so good he doesn't do all the cooking at his restaurant anymore. He has cooks who work for him. But he still makes the sauces and plans the menus. The only thing he won't tell me is the recipe for his super-great tomato sauce. He says he'll take that to his grave: it's a secret family recipe. (He gets a little dramatic sometimes, like me. I've decided my dramatic part is the Italian half of me.)

So last Wednesday night I knew he'd help me.

I'd decided to make three or four desserts for Gramma Rosa's birthday party. She really likes sweets, and she'd invited several of her friends. But that's when I ran into trouble. We were out of mascarpone.

Tiramisu, a rich Italian pudding-and-cake combination, requires mascarpone. Most important, it's Gramma's favorite dessert. She always orders it when we eat at Baldacci's.

"Mom," I said, pulling my Seahawks sweatshirt over my head, "I'm going to see Mr. B. It's an emergency. I'll be right back. Promise."

"It's so much harder to get away with killing people now that the police and FBI have these new forensics tests," Mom muttered, her nose deep in *The Complete Book of Poisons*. "They can identify almost any poison."

She wasn't listening to me. She was plotting.

"*Mom*!"

She glanced up.

"Why don't you kill him with a cake knife?"

"Fingerprints, Mikki. You know that. There'd be fingerprints."

"Have the killer wear gloves." I thought wildly. "Inside his armor." (I was supposed to be writing a paper on the Middle Ages for history.)

"If I could find a reason for Frankie to attend a Renaissance Fair ..." She scribbled something on the yellow pad she uses for plotting. "Did you say you were going somewhere?"

"To see Mr. B."

"It's after dinner. On a school night," she reminded me. As if I didn't know. "And don't talk to strangers!"

If I ever get married, which I probably won't have time to do because famous chefs work very long hours, Mom will tell me not to talk to strangers as I leave on my honeymoon. "I'll be right back. It's super important." I was out the door before she'd nodded.

Chapter 2

Seeing Mr. B during dinner hours presented two challenges. First, I had to get around Tiffany, the blonde pit bull in three inch heels who's the restaurant's hostess. And, second, I had to avoid the old guys in black suits who hung out in Baldacci's back room. They always stopped talking when I came near them. That was rude. I didn't want to hear their old stories anyway.

Wednesday night I wasn't going to let either of those obstacles stop me.

"Mikki. How nice to see you." Tiffany's fingernails were long and red, and her blouses were always too small. Maybe that was to show off the red heart tattooed right above her left boob. "Would you like to be seated?" She snapped a picture of me, the camera flash so close it blinded me. I walked right into the corner of the reception desk, banging my elbow. Hard.

"I'd like to see Mr. B. Please." I rubbed my elbow. It felt like wasps had used me for target practice.

"Mr. Baldacci can't be disturbed during dinner hours, dear."

"It's important. It's about Gramma Rosa."

My elbow throbbed. It would be a gorgeous purple by morning.

"Is she ill, Mikki? Is there a problem?" Tiffany purred sweetly.

"There will be if I can't see Mr. B." I smiled back. Not as sweetly.

"Why don't you come back tomorrow afternoon, when he isn't as busy?" She turned to a couple who'd just arrived. "Would you like to wait in the bar until a table is available?" Click, click. She'd taken pictures of the newcomers.

"I have to go to the ladies' room," I said, making an end run around Tiffany and cutting through the bar. Who would stop a girl desperate to pee?

The bathrooms were past a series of large paintings of Italy. They were also near the stairs leading down to Mr. B's office.

When he said he wasn't to be disturbed he couldn't have meant by me.

I stopped at the bottom of the stairs. Someone inside his office was yelling.

"Tony, you must have the dough."

"I don't. I swear to you! I never had it." Mr. B sounded really upset.

"Sal and you was tight. He trusted you like a brother. Tito and I figured it was you all these years, sending us the cash. I got no savings, Tony."

I leaned toward the half-open door. Grampa — the grandfather Mom said I wasn't supposed to talk about – was named Salvatore. Was he the "Sal" they were talking about?

"It wasn't me. I'm telling you. I don't know who it was. If you need money, what about getting a job?"

"I had a job, working for Sal! Kind of work I do doesn't exactly come with benefit packages. Who's gonna hire a guy like me? Most of my references are in God's hands."

"I'm sorry, Angelo. I can't help you."

"Rumor has it you're gonna make some changes around here. Changes requirin' big bucks. You expect us to believe that has nothin' to do with our cash flow drying up?" The voice was getting even angrier.

My whole body tightened. I moved closer to the office so I wouldn't miss anything.

"I was never involved with Sal's business. You and I've been friends too long to fight about this." That was Mr. B.

"Friends too long is right, Tony. Too long for you to hold out on me!"

The office door crashed open and Angelo Serio, one of the old guys who hung out in the private back room, stomped out.

His stomach flopped over the top of his pants and his face was covered with angry red blotches. He stormed toward the narrow staircase where I was standing.

I squeezed myself tighter against the wall, willing myself to be invisible.

Either Mr. Serio didn't notice I was there, or he thought I was just a short person who took a wrong turn on the way to the ladies' room. No one important enough to pay attention to.

He stomped up the stairway and across the dining room floor toward the back room. As soon as I was sure he wasn't coming back I knocked on the open office door. Mr. Baldacci was standing behind his desk, pouring himself a glass of Grappa. (That's Italian brandy.)

"Mikki! What are you doing here on a Wednesday night?" He took a small bottle out of the top drawer of his desk, shook out a pill, and swallowed it with a gulp.

"I need to borrow a pound of mascarpone cheese."

He started to laugh.

This was the Mr. B I knew.

"And so what am I? The local Italian grocer, that I should give you a pound of my best mascarpone?"

"Gramma Rosa's seventy-sixth birthday dessert party is Friday night. I want to make tiramisu, and the supermarket didn't have mascarpone."

"Psh. Supermarkets never have decent mascarpone." He waved his arms at me as if he was batting the supermarket away, like a mosquito. "Supermarkets are okay for cheddar and Swiss, but for a fine cheese such as mascarpone you need a shop that specializes in the best." He looked closely at me, and winked. "Unless, my little chef, you're lucky enough to have a certain friend down the street who has his own Italian kitchen."

Mr. B was passionate about what he served at his restaurant. He always said, "Fine food starts with fine ingredients."

"So you'll help me?" I asked. "Please?"

"I will consider doing so," he said, coming out from behind the desk. "On one condition only."

"Yes?" I asked, as he led me into the restaurant's pantry.

"That I be issued an invitation to this birthday dessert party for my dear friend Mrs. Rosa D'Andrea, and that you allow me also to bring a dessert."

I put out my hand to shake his. "It's a deal, Mr. B."

"Then I shall be at your home Friday night and I shall bring my Gelato di nocciola, which I personally know to be one of your grandmother's favorites."

"That's ...?" "Gelato" was Italian ice cream, but I didn't understand the rest.

"Italian hazelnut ice cream," he beamed. "I shall make my very best. And," he leaned close to me, "Friday night might also be the exact right time to make a very special announcement!"

Chapter 3

"Mom, please. You need to clean your papers off the couch and get dressed for the party. Gramma Rosa is changing her clothes. The guests will be here any minute!"

Mom nodded, but kept scribbling in her notebook. She was working out the details of a car chase in which Frankie, having survived his wife's attempt to poison him, is driven off a steep mountain road by his mistress. Frankie had problems.

"I'm going to add hemlock to my chocolate milk," I called back over my shoulder just to see if Mom was listening. I read her books on poisons, too.

"Hemlock works too fast, Mikki. You'll die and miss the party." Mom grinned and started gathering her papers. "And I'm going, I'm going." She peeked in the kitchen. "Your desserts look spectacular!" I hadn't seen her smile like that since before Dad left.

Maybe there was hope.

In the meantime, there were desserts.

All of the guests were Gramma Rosa's age, of course. I was probably the youngest person they'd talked to in thirty years.

A few of them had trouble walking, like Gramma, but no one had problems eating my desserts. I refilled the platter of raspberry filled miniature cream puffs three times. Mr. B's hazelnut ice cream was as fantastic as he'd promised, and, thanks to his mascarpone, so was my tiramisu. Mom put seven large candles (for decades) and six small ones (for regular years) on the German Black Forest cake. Gramma Rosa blew them all out in one breath.

Her arthritis might be bad, but her lungs were fine.

Then everyone sang "Happy Birthday" really loud and off-key, just the way it should be sung.

I was so busy serving seconds and thirds of the desserts I didn't have time to think about the largish burn on the top of my hand, and no one else noticed it. I'd managed to hit the top oven rack while I was taking the chocolate cake out of the oven. Scorched skin hurts, even if you pour cold water over it. And, as predicted, my elbow was now shades of lavender from whamming the reception desk at Baldacci's Wednesday night. I wore a long-sleeved tee shirt to cover it.

If I'd been in Seattle Dad would have noticed the burn for sure. He'd have lectured me about kitchen safety. Then he'd have hugged me and told me how delicious the food was. Mom would have sighed and said, "Please be more careful, Mikki." I would have been banned from the kitchen and we'd have been forced to survive on take-out for a few days.

Can you imagine a basketball star being banned from holding a basketball for ten days just because he slipped on the court? Professional chefs have to ignore little accidents like cuts from chopping onions or scrapes from grating cheese or burns from the chocolate cake. I'm totally fine with that. All great chefs have battle wounds.

But injuries on behalf of accomplishments should be recognized. Tonight, no one noticed my hand.

By nine o'clock everyone had left except Mom, Gramma Rosa, Mr. B and me.

It was finally quiet enough so I could ask the question I'd kept thinking about. "Mr. B, why was Mr. Serio yelling at you Wednesday night? Why did he say you should give him money?"

Mr. B stopped smiling. "Your ears were too far open. You shouldn't have heard that. Angelo's an old friend who's having hard times. Nothing for you to worry about."

He and Gramma Rosa exchanged looks.

Gramma Rosa took another sip of her third glass of wine. Then she clapped her hands. "It's time, Tony," she said, "We've waited long enough."

"You're sure, Rosa? No longer a secret?"

"Not a secret. A celebration. Tell them!"

"Excellent! Then here is our announcement," said Mr. Baldacci, standing and raising his glass. "In the past year Baldacci's has been doing so well we've had to turn customers away. It has hurt me to say 'there is no room at my tables,' to old friends. It has been my dream to expand: to build a larger dining room and more modern kitchen." He smiled at Gramma Rosa as though they were young sweethearts sharing news of their engagement. "Tonight we announce my dear friend Mrs. Rosa D'Andrea has agreed to be my silent partner in such a venture."

"Mother? You're investing in the restaurant?" said Mom. "Isn't that risky?"

"At seventy-six, being able to invest in the dream of an old friend isn't a risk," said Gramma Rosa. "It's a blessing. We have it all figured. Papers are signed. We have an architect and a builder. Can you believe that with my mouth I'm going to be a 'silent partner'? Tony will run the restaurant as always. The bigger and better Baldacci's Restaurant will bring in new customers."

"Wow!" I said.

"The plans are in my office. I've kept them hidden until everything was official. After we close tonight I'll tell my staff, and we'll share a little Grappa to celebrate. No longer a secret." He smiled again at Gramma Rosa.

"But to expand the restaurant at your age. That's a lot of work," Mom pointed out.

"You sound like my son, Luc. He says, 'You're getting older. Consider your heart. You should slow down. Think about retiring.' That's why I haven't told him our plans. What would I do if I had no Baldacci's Restaurant to go to every day? I get up before dawn to go to markets in New York and pick the very best fish and meats. I'm at the restaurant by six every morning, and stay after midnight to make sure all is prepared for the next day. Baldacci's is my life. I will never give it up as long as I am breathing!"

"Nevertheless, Tony, you must call Luc and tell him and Bambi your plans," said Gramma Rosa. "Before you tell your staff, tell your family."

"Rosa, Rosa, I'll do it. I promise. I only hope Luc's the one to answer, and not that wife of his. Bambi, I could do without. Why my son married someone named after a baby deer I will never understand. I even hired that floozy friend of hers to be my hostess, and still Bambi calls to ask me crazy questions."

"Relax, Tony. Tell Bambi it's a Friday night and you can't talk. You have customers to take care of," advised Gramma Rosa.

"Will you close Baldacci's during the construction?" I asked.

"For a short time only," said Mr. B. "The addition will be built, and then we'll close a week or two while we attach the old building to the new."

"It's all planned, you see?" said Gramma Rosa. "It's not going to look like the old Baldacci's. Everything will be up-to-date and modern."

"But with the same delicious food!" said Mr. B. "Which I had better get back to the restaurant to check on now. But before that I have a special gift to bestow." Mr. B pulled a shopping bag out from behind the couch. He must have hidden it there on his way in.

"Tony, I'm too old for birthday gifts," said Gramma Rosa."

"And who said this was for you?" he said. He handed the bag to me. "I've waited many years to hand this on to someone who would appreciate it, and life has finally delivered that person to me. This gift is for Miss Michelle Norden, future chef and delightful young friend."

What could he be giving me? A recipe book? Something to use in the kitchen? The bag was heavy, but it didn't feel like a book.

"So, open it!" he said. "Time is passing! Why keep us waiting?"

I tore the butcher's paper off what was inside. It was an old discolored pewter figure of a robed man holding a grill. Not exactly a gift a girl dreams of. I tried not to seem disappointed, and looked at Mr. B, questioningly.

"So? You recognize him?" he asked hopefully.

For his sake, I wished I did. But I had no idea who the pewter man was.

"He's Saint Lawrence," Mr. B said, plainly disappointed I didn't recognize him. "Patron saint of chefs. My father gave this very statue to me for luck on the night I opened my first restaurant. And luck I've had! Now I've decided to pass that luck on to you, my young friend. Someday you will be a very special chef, and perhaps you, too, will have your own restaurant, and Saint Lawrence will oversee *your* kitchen, as he has mine."

"Thank you, Mr. B." I hugged Saint Lawrence, and then, when I saw the tears in Mr. B's eyes, hugged him, too. "I'll treasure him, always, because he came from you."

I looked at the statue again. "Why is Saint Lawrence holding a grill?"

"Because he was roasted to death," Mr. B answered, smiling.

"Saint Lawrence had so much faith in God he joked with his enemies and told them, 'I am roasted enough on this side; perhaps now you should turn me over!'"

Gross.

I wished I hadn't asked about the grill.

Then Mr. B hugged Gramma Rosa and Mom and kissed all of us on our cheeks and left.

Dad's relatives back in Seattle aren't big huggers, but Mom's New Jersey family and friends get pretty emotional. I kind of like it.

Mom looked at Gramma Rosa. "Mother, are you sure investing in a restaurant is what you want to do with your money?"

"Very sure," said Gramma Rosa. "It was my idea, not Tony's. Not to worry, Cate. Trust me. I have the money. Now, why don't you help my newly seventy-six-year-old bones get themselves to bed?"

Mom just shook her head and helped Gramma toward her bedroom, leaving me to put the food away and the dishes in the dishwasher.

I managed to finish off a couple of raspberry-filled creampuffs along the way. If you don't eat them right away they get soggy.

Dad would have said, "There are people starving in the world." Unfortunately for them, they were never around when I had leftovers.

It had been an excellent birthday party.

Plus, now I had the luck of Saint Lawrence on my side. And we were going to have a restaurant in the family! Right then, being in New Jersey seemed pretty terrific. Even if Dad was almost three thousand miles away.

Before I went to bed I cleared a space above the cookbooks in my bookcase for my statue. When I did talk to Dad, the first thing I'd tell him about was Mr. B's gift.

If I'd known what was going to happen I might have told Mr. B he should keep his lucky Saint Lawrence a little while longer. But how could I have known?

I went to bed with my favorite recipe book and fell asleep next to Cat before I even got to the baking section.

Chapter 4

I woke up at five forty-two Saturday morning, starved.

Mom had left her books on criminal behavior and forensics all over the living room again. She'd also left a note on the kitchen table:

*Mikki – Forgot to tell you! I managed to get to a gourmet cheese store yesterday. A pound of mascarpone is on the second shelf of the frig so you can replace what you borrowed from Mr. Baldacci. Your desserts rated ***** (five stars!) tonight! Love, Mom*

Five stars was like an A+ in school!

I hummed as I decided what I wanted for breakfast. I'd been so busy cooking and serving at Gramma Rosa's party the night before that all I'd eaten were a few bites of each dessert. Delicious, yes. Filling? Not so much.

I cut myself a generous hunk of leftover German chocolate cake. (Tasting is a big perk of being a cook. You also get to plan the menu, so you can make sure your favs are on the table. At my house you will never be served tofu. Or okra. Or rutabagas.)

I became our full-time cook years ago, when I realized that if Mom was in charge of the kitchen we'd live on take-out and frozen pizzas and probably all die at early ages of vitamin deficiencies. I was about eight then.

It wasn't that Mom couldn't cook. Cooking just wasn't her highest priority.

Writing mysteries was.

If you put together all the books she's written she's probably killed off two or three dozen people. You could even call her a serial killer. Of course, all those people were fictional.

To inspire her, we watch crime shows on TV, and DVDs of her favorites, like *The Sopranos*, and movies like *Rebecca* and *Rear Window* and *Murder on the Orient Express*. My favorite (of course) is *Who is Killing the Great Chefs of Europe?* I've seen them all. Many times.

I suspect not many moms consult their daughters about places to hide bodies, or let their kids read books about how to kill people. (The books on poisons are my favorites. They're sort of "Cooking for Killers".) My mom says learning is a good thing, no matter what the subject.

Unfortunately, she's not a big deal best-selling author. Not yet. She's gotten a stack of rejection e-mails and letters (she papered the upstairs bathroom with them in Seattle) but she still hasn't had a book published. A bottle of champagne had been in our Seattle refrigerator, waiting to be opened when she sold her first book. Once in a while Mom would take it out, dust it off, and look at it.

Now there's a bottle in the refrigerator here.

I understand, because I want to be a chef as much as Mom wants to be published. Maybe more. I just hope my food doesn't get rejected as many times as her books have been.

That's why I study cookbooks, and want to go to a cooking school. Unfortunately, I have to pass ninth grade history before I can graduate from high school and get on a plane to Paris or Rome, where the best cooking schools are.

Which is why I planned to spend Saturday at the library researching the history paper that's due next Monday. Mr. Morelli requires students to use at least two encyclopedias, three books, and one magazine or newspaper article for each paper. He believes, and here I quote, "Google is not the answer to the world's questions." Writing a paper for his class is sort of like researching the Middle Ages as though you were living in the Middle Ages.

But the Victoria Public Library in Edgewood wouldn't open for hours.

While I was savoring my (second) piece of chocolate cake, I had a brilliant idea. Mr. B was probably already at his restaurant. Hadn't he said last night that he was there by six every morning? I could take the replacement mascarpone to him now.

I wrote a note to Mom telling her where I'd be, pulled my cozy gray University of Washington sweatshirt over my head, and tied my hair back in sort of a ponytail to keep it off my face.

I never looked in a mirror and saw anyone I was. The girl in the mirror was tall and skinny with straight brown hair, usually parted unevenly, and a broad nose. No one I could possibly be. So I avoided mirrors. But in Gramma Rosa's house it's impossible to escape them. I glanced in the hall mirror on my way out.

I still hadn't changed into a raving beauty. But I kept hoping.

Edgewood streets were deserted this early on a Saturday morning. The only sounds were the scrunch of the first dry orange and yellow leaves under my feet. Another couple of weeks and I'd be hearing leaf-blowers instead of birds. The air had that crisp smell that said, "Fall."

Pumpkins and pots of chrysanthemums were on almost every front porch and cornstalk wreaths hung on front doors.

Two dogs barked, one after the other. A crow cawed three times. Another answered. (Did you know that a flock of crows is called a murder?)

All was peaceful.

Until I heard feet pounding on the pavement. Someone was running. Coming closer.

Closer.

I stopped.

My heart pumped faster.

The sound got louder.

I was near the corner of Drew and Taylor.

I looked in back of me. Then ahead.

No one was on Drew.

The feet were getting closer.

Chase scenes from Mom's books flashed in front of me.

What if a masked man attacked me? What if he had a knife? A gun?

Should I run? How could I escape?

On my right a tall hedge separated two houses.

A place to hide?

I ran toward it, dodging past the carefully trimmed bushes edging the front walk. I'd almost made it to the hedge when my feet slipped out from under me. Down …

I was sprawled in a pile of soggy leaves. Smelly leaves. Those dogs might have been there before me. I closed my eyes and cursed silently. Peppercorns!

The running feet were almost on top of me.

I was fated to die right here in Edgewood, New Jersey. I could see the headline. "New Girl in Town Dies in Pile of Dog Poop."

The steps stopped.

I opened my left eye and looked up. Then I opened my right eye.

"Hey! Are you okay?" A boy stood above me, breathing hard.

I checked. All my various parts seemed to work. "I guess so." I got up, carefully.

He was staring at my legs. "People are such slobs. They're supposed to clean up after their dogs."

I looked down. Sure enough. My nose had not lied. Massive quantities of dog poop were all over my left shoe and leg. Gross. I reached down and tried to rub it off with leaves. Not a pretty picture. Or aroma.

"You're the new girl. Mikki something."

By that time I figured I wasn't being murdered or mugged. Just mortified.

He was the cute guy who sat in the row next to me in history class. Richard. And now he was talking. To me.

"Mikki Norden," I managed to reply. "Why were you running?" I kept desperately brushing my leg and foot with wet leaves, hoping he wouldn't notice how red my face was. The first time someone my own age in this town had actually talked to me, and I'm stinky with dog poop.

"Coach said I might make it onto the high school track team next year if I worked out more," Richard was ignoring my efforts to clean myself up. He had his head down, his hands on his knees, and was breathing heavily. "I run most mornings." He stood up straight. "What were *you* doing? Before you slipped?"

I pulled the now somewhat-mashed package of mascarpone out of my sweatshirt pocket. "Taking cheese to Baldacci's. I borrowed some from Mr. B the other day."

"You're returning cheese at six o'clock in the morning?"

I shrugged. "I was awake, and he gets to the restaurant early."

"Oh." He looked dubious.

We both just stood there. Richard shuffled his feet a little. "I've about finished my run. Mind if I go with you? I need to walk to cool off."

"I guess." He wanted to walk with *me*? Had he confused me with someone else?

We took the short cut toward Main Street and walked around the strip mall. No businesses were open this early. Neither of us said anything for a while. I finally came up with,

"Aren't you on the soccer team?"

"Yeah. But high school soccer is pretty much nothing. The best players are in regional leagues, not on the public school team. I think track's more my sport."

"So why do you hang with those guys?"

"They're not really my friends. We're just on the same team." He changed the subject. "What're you doing your Middle Ages paper on?"

"The Children's Crusade."

"Cool. People thought those kids could march to the Holy Lands and be victorious because they were young and innocent. Instead, most of them died or were sold into slavery. Right?"

"Something like that." I hadn't actually read much about the Children's Crusade yet. I'd just circled it on a list of suggested topics. "What're you writing about?"

"Building castles. How men cut the stones, moved them, and then lifted them without all the machinery we have now."

"I never thought about that." I never had, actually.

"So why'd you borrow cheese from a restaurant?"

"Mr. B's a friend of mine. The supermarket didn't have the kind of cheese I needed."

"You were cooking?"

"Making tiramisu."

"Making *what?*"

"An Italian dessert. Really rich."

Richard looked doubtful. "You cook?"

"It's kind of my thing. Like your thing is track."

Richard nodded. "You should have chosen a topic for history class about cooking."

"I tried. Mr. Morelli said we don't know enough about cooking in the Middle Ages for me to write a paper on it. He probably thought I was going to try to kill and roast a boar and bring it in for show and tell."

"That would be cool! More fun than writing a paper!"

We grinned at each other. At least Richard didn't think it was strange that I cooked. A few kids in Seattle thought it was weird I was more interested in cookbooks than books about wizards or vampires or mythological gods.

The front door of Baldacci's was locked.

"It doesn't open until 11:30 for lunch on Saturdays." Richard read the sign. "Your friend probably doesn't want people wandering through his restaurant before then."

"His van is here," I said, pointing. It was parked at the side of the lot. "He must have used the back door."

Large bushes hid the door of the loading dock from the main parking lot. I'd only been back there once before. It was unlocked.

We stepped into the hallway leading to the kitchen, the pantry, and Mr. B's office. "Hello? Mr. B?" My voice echoed.

"Maybe he's upstairs in the restaurant," suggested Richard.

"Maybe."

Crash! The whole building shook. It felt as though the second floor was collapsing on top of us.

We both jumped. And then froze.

"He must be upstairs," Richard whispered.

"Unless there's a ghost in the restaurant," I added, trying to joke.

We looked at each other and headed for the stairs.

We didn't get far. As we passed Mr. B's office we saw him on the floor, his face a bright red. Papers were scattered around him, as though he'd wiped them off his desk as he'd fallen.

Richard got to him first. "Call 911. My dad taught me CPR, in case anyone had a heart attack at his dojang." He knelt and started pushing down on Mr. B's chest.

I picked up the telephone and tried to speak without my voice shaking. "Please. We need an ambulance. Right away. Baldacci's restaurant on Main Street in Edgewood. The back entrance."

Chapter 5

Edgewood Police Chief Weston Hunter put down his notebook and looked at Richard and me. "What were you two kids doing here at six in the morning anyway? Wanted pizza for breakfast or something?"

Neither of us smiled.

"Mr. B's dead, isn't he?" I asked quietly. I was trying very hard not to cry, but one tear was running down my cheek. I brushed it away with the side of my hand. The ambulance team had taken my friend away on a stretcher, but the expressions on their faces had been pretty grim.

"I tried CPR," said Richard. "I guess it didn't help."

Chief Hunter picked up a bottle of pills that had spilled onto the desk. "He was taking nitroglycerin pills. Looks to me as though he had a heart attack. You did your best." He put his hand on Richard's shoulder. "He was lucky you were here to try to help. Probably no one could have saved him. But you still haven't told me what you were doing here."

"I was replacing his mascarpone," I sniffed, pointing to the small package I'd dropped on the visitor's chair. "I borrowed some from him Wednesday night."

"At six on a Saturday morning?" Chief Hunter looked dubious.

"Well, go put that stuff in the restaurant refrigerator. You know where it is?" He stopped. "And what is that I smell?"

"It's … ah … my leg. I'm going to the ladies' room. On my way to the refrigerator."

"Wait! Before you go." Chief Hunter picked up his notebook again. "Richard, I know you. I took one of your dad's self-defense classes three years ago. But who are you, young lady? For the record."

"Mikki Norden. Michelle Norden. I moved here from Seattle six weeks ago."

He nodded. "Okay. What's your address, Mikki?"

"159 North Claremont Street."

Chief Hunter started to write and then looked up. "You're one of the D'Andreas?"

That name. But I couldn't very well lie to the police, could I? "Rosa D'Andrea's my grandmother."

Chief Hunter stared at me. Hard. "You're Cate D'Andrea's daughter?"

"Her name is Cate Norden now."

"Cate and I went to high school together. I didn't know she was back in town. Were any other members of your family here this morning?" He actually looked around as though I'd hidden Mom or Gramma Rosa under the desk.

Richard spoke up. "Mikki and I were the only ones here. And Mr. Baldacci, of course."

Chief Hunter kept looking at me, a little strangely. "Okay. For now. I have your names and addresses in case I think of more questions."

"What will happen?" I asked him. "Who will tell Mr. B's son that he's dead?"

"According to that prescription bottle Baldacci was a patient of Doctor Breeden's, right here in town. I'll give the doc a call. Either he or I will call his son right away. Don't you worry about that. Just get on back to your homes." I picked up the cheese, and Richard and I started moving toward the door. "And thank you. You did the right thing this morning. You tried to save Mr. Baldacci and you called for help."

I looked around again. Mr. B was really dead. It had happened so quickly. Mom wrote about death in her books, but this was the first time I'd come close to it in real life. This wasn't like in stories. It wasn't exciting or mysterious. It was sad. And empty.

I headed for the bathroom and scrubbed the dog poop off my shoe and leg with paper towels, and then went to the kitchen. Richard followed me as I put my mascarpone with the other cheeses in the big stainless steel restaurant refrigerator. We went out the service entrance and walked slowly through the parking lot toward the street.

"Wait." Richard stopped. "Wasn't the front door of the restaurant locked when we got here?"

"Definitely," I agreed.

Now the door was ajar.

"Did any of the EMTs or the police use that door?" he asked.

"I don't think so," I answered. "The ambulance came to the back door."

The front door was definitely unlocked now. We looked at each other and slipped inside.

The restaurant was arranged as it always was before it opened: tables set and waiting for customers. Usually at the far end of the bar a heavy open cabinet was stacked with clean glasses.

Not this morning. Now that cabinet was lying on its side. Thick bar glasses, some broken and some still intact, were scattered over the floor. Slivers and chunks of broken glass lay everywhere. I peeked behind the bar. An empty cup was in the small sink.

"That crash we heard, just after we came in," I remembered.

"Someone else was in the restaurant," Richard agreed.

"And left by the front door," I added. "We have to tell the chief."

We ran down the back stairs to where we'd left Chief Hunter, but he wasn't there. His police car wasn't in the parking lot. He'd already left.

Was it important that someone else had been in the building when Mr. Baldacci had a heart attack?

"If someone else was here, why didn't *they* call 911?" I asked. "Why did they leave the building?"

Chapter 6

We walked slowly back toward the mall.

I kept thinking of Mr. B lying there, dead, next to his desk.

"I was wondering," Richard said. "I mean, I got up early and ran, and then being in the restaurant and everything. I'm kind of hungry."

"Food?" I asked bluntly. Was he really talking about food? At a time like this?

"My mom is visiting her sister in New York this weekend, and since you're such a good cook and all, if maybe you ..."

"You want me to cook breakfast for you? When my dearest friend in the whole world just died?" Ninety-nine days out of a hundred I'd love to cook. Especially for someone who was as cute as Richard and who was actually talking to me. But this morning? He had to be kidding.

"I guess it's a bad idea."

I sighed. "No. It's okay. Maybe cooking will help me get my mind off ..."

"Can you make pancakes?" Richard looked hopeful.

A magazine headline I once saw at the dentist's office said men have only one thing on their minds. I'm pretty sure that one thing is their stomach. Richard had just been giving CPR to a dead man. Now he was thinking about pancakes.

Mom was up, awake, and grinding coffee beans. Making coffee was one kitchen task she hadn't given up. Mystery writing requires the availability of strong black coffee twenty-four hours a day, and I wasn't always around. Like, I had to go to school. Brewing coffee was Mom's job.

"Mikki! And you've brought a friend!" She pulled the sash of her white terry cloth bathrobe (covered with pictures of little red skeletons and yellow crime scene tape) tighter. "I saw your note. I didn't expect visitors so early on a Saturday morning."

"This is Richard. He's in my history class." I realized I didn't know his last name.

"Pleased to meet you," he said. He held out his hand for Mom to shake. I could tell he was trying not to stare at her bathrobe. It was probably the only one like it in Edgewood. "I'm Richard Park. My dad owns Park's Taekwondo Dojang, down in the mall."

"I've seen the sign there. I've thought maybe Mikki and I should take self-defense classes."

Yuck, Mom. Don't overdo it. Just what we need. Mother and daughter classes with Richard's dad.

"Dad's classes for women are very popular," Richard said. "I'll get Mikki a brochure listing them."

"Mom, something awful happened," I interrupted, before she'd signed us both up. I told her about Mr. Baldacci.

"You were there? You found him?" She sat down at the kitchen table, holding her coffee mug as if it were a lifeline. "He was such a wonderful man." She looked at me speculatively. "It was your first dead body, wasn't it, Mikki? How did you feel? And how did he look? Was the body in rigor yet? Were his eyes open? What exactly did the paramedics do?"

Richard's eyes opened wider.

"Not now, Mom. Can we talk later?" I took an egg out of the

refrigerator, separated it, and started whipping the white. "Why don't you go tell Gramma Rosa?"

"Right," she nodded, as she left the kitchen. If Mr. Baldacci's body had been a crime scene Mom would've been asking questions for hours. Research, you know. If we go out for dinner she takes notes on conversations at the next table.

See why I've never asked to have a slumber party at my house? She'd probably hide a tape recorder in back of a potted plant and record the whole event as notes for the Y.A. book she may write some day. Or there'd be a slumber party in her next mystery, complete with the mass murder of all my friends. And, just my luck, that would be the book that'd be published.

Sung Ja had known me forever. She'd understood. But I had no idea how Richard would like having his words turn up as dialog in one of Mom's manuscripts.

I didn't want him knowing how strange Mom was before I'd even gotten to know him.

I added milk, melted butter, lemon juice, and a generous tablespoon of maple syrup, my secret ingredient, to the yolk and stirred it all together. Hard. I'd been stirring for several minutes before I realized I was overdoing the stirring a bit because I was trying not to cry.

I wiped my eyes, took a deep breath, and mixed in the dry ingredients.

"What are you cooking, Mikki?" Mom appeared back in the doorway of the kitchen.

"Blueberry pancakes," I said, checking the freezer to make sure we still had some of the wild blueberries I'd used in muffins two weeks ago. We did. "Richard hasn't had breakfast. His mother's out of town." I gave Mom a meaningful look. "He was a big help this morning." I didn't add, *and he's pretty much the only person my age who's spoken to me since we moved to New Jersey.*

Mom got the message. "Good idea. I'll see how your grandmother is doing."

I heated the griddle.

Richard sat down at the table. He didn't mention Mom's bathrobe or her questions. Or my obvious efforts not to cry. "Where did you live before you moved here?"

"Seattle. But my mom grew up here in Edgewood."

"I heard Chief Hunter say he knew her in high school. Weird."

"Very weird," I agreed. Was it good or bad to have someone you knew a long time ago now be chief of police? Mom probably would think it was cool. He could be a great research source.

As soon as the griddle was the right temperature I poured out the first four pancakes. "We came back to New Jersey to help take care of my grandmother." That was the official reason for our move. Richard didn't need to know Dad deserted us.

Richard nodded. "Just you and your mom?"

I didn't look at him. "My dad stayed in Seattle."

Luckily, he didn't ask any more questions.

While the second side of the pancakes was browning I put plates and butter on the table, and warmed maple syrup in the microwave. Nothing's worse than cold maple syrup on warm pancakes. Well, almost nothing. "Have you always lived here?"

"Forever. I was even born in Edgewood Hospital. It must be great to start fresh in a new place."

"I guess," I said. I put the first pancakes on Richard's plate and poured batter for another four onto the griddle.

"In a new place no one would know you puked on your first Cub Scout overnight, or struck out in the key inning of the Little League Championship game." He took several bites of the pancakes. "These are terrific, Mikki!"

"Thank you." Every cook likes to be appreciated.

I kept cooking. Richard kept eating. I made enough for Mom and Gramma Rosa, too. Richard helped himself to another four.

"I still can't believe Mr. Baldacci's dead," I said. "He was here last night, at my grandmother's birthday party. He was so excited; Gramma Rosa was going to be his partner, and they were going to build an addition to the restaurant." I'd finished cooking the pancakes and was eating one myself. They weren't bad, even made with frozen blueberries. Fresh are best.

Mr. B told me that.

I blinked back another tear.

Richard polished off his twelfth or thirteenth pancake. "I'll really miss his special pizza. Even if the restaurant stays open it won't be the same."

I nodded. What *would* happen? Gramma Rosa was a silent partner. Did Mr. B's death mean part of the restaurant was hers? He'd probably left everything to his son. Was Gramma Rosa now his son's partner?

"At least the guy must have died eating some of his favorite foods," Richard said, looking hopefully at the pancakes I'd put aside for Mom and Gramma Rosa.

"What do you mean?" I asked. "I didn't see any food in his office. Just half a cup of coffee."

"I smelled his breath, when I was giving him CPR," said Richard. "He stank of almonds."

"Almonds?" I almost dropped my spatula. "Are you sure?"

"The nose knows," Richard said, tapping his. "I love nuts. Almonds are my favs."

"We need to tell the police," I said, getting up and reaching for the kitchen telephone. "Right away."

"What? Are you crazy? Tell the police the man ate a few farewell nuts?"

I turned back toward him. "Did you see any nuts in his office? Cyanide smells like almonds, Richard. Mr. B was poisoned."

Chapter 7

Before I could explain the facts of death by cyanide poisoning to Richard, Mom came back into the kitchen.

She'd put on jeans and a sweater and tied a scarf around her long hair. Mom's idea of dressing for company was putting on lipstick.

"I told Gramma Rosa about Mr. Baldacci. She says she needs to see her lawyer immediately. I can't talk her out of it." Mom looked flustered. She picked up a now-room-temperature pancake and absent-mindedly dipped it in maple syrup. Three drips of the syrup made a line down her sweater. She didn't notice them until I wet a paper towel and patted her clean. "This is exactly why I didn't want to come back to live in New Jersey."

I didn't think she meant the maple syrup.

Then Mom remembered we had a guest. "I can drop you at your house on our way, Richard."

"Thanks, Mrs. Norden. I should shower and get out of my running clothes. Maybe I'll see you at the library later, Mikki? I'll be in the reference room."

Was he asking to meet me there? Like a real friend would? "I was going there later to work on my history paper. I'll pull my notes together and head downtown." Did I sound too eager? But aside from wanting an excuse to see Richard again, concentrating on homework today wouldn't be easy. Seeing a friendly face at the library would help.

All I could think was, "Mr. B was murdered."

Gramma Rosa appeared, hair immaculate, make-up in place, and clomping her walker at high speed. She didn't stop for pancakes.

After she and Mom and Richard disappeared I took a long look at the telephone. Should I call Chief Hunter to make sure he asked the medical examiner to check for cyanide poisoning?

No. I wouldn't interfere. Mr. B's autopsy would show he'd been poisoned.

If not, I'd go to the police in person.

Chapter 8

Richard was sitting in the Reference Room surrounded by books on architecture and castles when I got to the library.

"I'm going to look for some source books for my paper," I whispered. I found two books that listed the children's crusade in their indexes. After I put them on the table I found a third book and the "C" volume in an encyclopedia.

Richard was scribbling notes and making little drawings. Clearly he was finding lots of information about castle construction.

"Richard!" I whispered to him five minutes later.

"What?"

"What should I do if the subject of my paper didn't happen?"

He looked at me as though I were a third grader. "Mikki, the Crusades happened."

"Right. The Crusades happened. But according to this book," I pointed to the first volume I'd looked at, "there were two children's crusades in 1212. One was led by a twelve year old boy in Germany, and one by a twelve year old boy in France."

"Interesting coincidence," said Richard. "So?"

"According to *this* book," I pointed to the second book, "there was no children's crusade. Not one. It says there was a famine in 1212. Starving people were wandering around Europe looking for food. Those boys in Germany and France led some of those people, so early historians thought they were children going on a crusade. People liked that idea, so they kept writing it down. History books include a Children's Crusade when maybe there never was one."

"Interesting!" Now Richard was paying attention. "Maybe that's why Mr. Morelli said we needed to check different sources. What does the encyclopedia say?"

"That we don't know if there really was a children's crusade. It might have happened. Or might not."

"Then that's what you write," said Richard decisively. "Say there are conflicting views." He reached over and looked at one of my books. "You're writing about the year 1212."

"Right."

"So you can't go back and interview people who were there." He paused. "It's like a mystery. Historians looked at the circumstantial evidence, put it together and called it a Children's Crusade."

"Exactly!" I said. "Like our finding Mr. Baldacci this morning. He was dead. And his heart pills were on his desk. So Chief Hunter assumed he'd had a heart attack." Richard loved history, but I was more interested in what had happened right here, today, in Edgewood.

"Yeah. But Chief Hunter was probably right. Mr. Baldacci was old. And he did have a heart condition."

"Circumstantial evidence!" I pointed out. "Chief Hunter jumped to a conclusion without all the evidence."

"Evidence?" said Richard.

"First, Mr. Baldacci smelled of almonds. You said so. That's a definite sign of cyanide poisoning. Second, we heard that crash upstairs. Someone was in the restaurant before we got there."

"It sounded that way," Richard admitted. "Maybe whoever was there got scared when they heard us and left. How do you know so much about cyanide, anyway?"

"My mom writes mysteries. We have all sorts of books on poisoning and forensics and stuff at home. Cyanide is a basic."

Richard rolled his eyes a little.

I ignored him. "If Chief Hunter knew the cabinet was knocked over while we were at the restaurant, maybe he'd look at Mr. Baldacci's death differently. Especially after he finds out Mr. Baldacci was poisoned."

"Or maybe he'll think we knocked over the cabinet," Richard pointed out. "Mikki, probably Mr. Baldacci just died. There's no mystery."

"But why would someone leave the restaurant just then? Unless they'd done something awful. Unless they were guilty … of murder!"

Chapter 9

"You've read too many of your mother's mysteries. Mr. Baldacci was your friend. But he was also an old man with a heart condition."

"What if *everyone* thinks that? What if the killer gets away? That happens, you know."

Richard shook his head and turned back to his books on castles.

Chief Hunter knew Richard, and Richard had been the one to smell the almonds. I couldn't go to the police without him.

But we were in a library. In a few minutes I found what I was looking for right there in the Reference Room.

I dropped the proof on top of his notebook. "Look at this," I whispered. I pointed to the list of "Heart Attack Symptoms" in the medical book I'd found. "Pale and Clammy Skin" was number three on the list. "You saw Mr. B closer than anyone else. What color was his skin?"

"Bright pink," Richard said softly. "Almost red. Definitely not pale."

I pulled that book away and opened the second book to the symptoms of "Cyanide Poisoning." "Cherry Red Skin" was second on the list, right above, "Almond-like odor."

Richard looked at me. "Chief Hunter will figure it out. On TV the police always figure out whether someone is murdered, and who did it."

I hated to break the news to Richard. Real life wasn't like TV.

Ding! Ding! I jumped. The grandfather clock in the corner of the reference room chimed. It kept going until it reached twelve "dings."

Richard stuffed his papers and notebook inside his backpack. "I promised Dad I'd rake leaves in our back yard this afternoon. See you in school Monday."

I sighed and went back to the Children's Crusade. Why should I write a paper on something that probably hadn't even happened? Because I needed at least a B in history, that's why.

A chef had to understand math and chemistry. That made sense. But when you were making the perfect soufflé, who cared what had happened (or not) eight hundred years ago?

Half an hour later I closed the history books and put them on the library cart next to the ones Richard had used.

I didn't want to go straight home. Mom and Gramma Rose would probably be there, talking about Mr. B. Should I tell them he'd been murdered? That would only upset Gramma Rosa and get Mom all excited about research possibilities.

I needed to think.

In the very center of Edgewood, next to the town hall and the police department, there's a little park. From a distance it looks like a great place to fly a kite or sit and read a book, but up close you can see the grass is covered in Canada Goose droppings. The geese are pretty, but they honk and spit and chase anyone who comes near the pond in the center of the park. They allow you to walk on the sidewalk around the park, but not on the grass. I learned that the very first week I lived here.

Maybe those geese had come from Canada originally, but they were definitely Jersey geese now. I watched them a while. They'd figured out how to control their new territory. How long had it taken them to feel at home here?

I headed toward the strip mall, to Edna's Diner. Edna's had booths on one side of the door, tables on the other, and a counter between them where you could sit and eat or order take-out.

A double chocolate chip ice cream cone with sprinkles would be a soothing lunch. I totally ignored all my usual concerns about nutrition. Today I needed a lot of chocolate.

Edna's was jammed with women taking a break from shopping, couples with noisy toddlers, divorced dads with kids ordering cheeseburgers, and giggling teenagers.

Then I saw someone I knew in the middle of the dining area. You know when you recognize someone, but you can't think who it is because the person is out of their usual place? Like, you see your dentist at the beach? Or your teacher at an amusement park? But when the waitress moved away from that table I connected like mad.

Mr. B's hostess, Tiffany, wearing one of her tight blouses, was with a tanning-booth bronzed older woman wearing enormous dark sunglasses. What was Tiffany doing at Edna's? Maybe she'd come for lunch because Baldacci's was closed. But maybe she knew something about Mr. Baldacci's death. When someone's murdered, everyone close to him or her is a suspect.

The high school girl behind the counter handed me my dangerously high, covered-with-sprinkles, double chocolate chip cone, and I had an inspired idea. Taking a fast lick and holding my cone high above the heads of the seated customers I wove my way through the tables and chairs and headed for Tiffany and her tablemate. The restaurant was incredibly noisy. Would I be able to hear anything they said?

I had to try.

I approached the table from Tiffany's rear, hoping she wouldn't notice me. At the next table a toddler in a high chair was stuffing French fries into his mouth and then spitting them out (gross) while his mother tried to eat a fruit plate and keep his big sister from dropping spaghetti onto her lap.

I was close enough to see Tiffany push her salad aside and sip a strawberry shake through a straw. She was listening intently to the woman in sunglasses. I moved around the highchair, hoping to overhear what they were saying.

No one paid attention to me until the munchkin with the spaghetti took one long look at my cone and screamed, "*Ice cream! Ice cream! I want ice cream! Now!*" His scream startled a waiter passing in back of me who stumbled, knocking against me, and pushing me just enough so my two scoops of double chocolate chip with extra sprinkles slipped from my cone and down, down, down the front of Tiffany's white blouse, sliding right on top of her little red tattooed heart.

She screamed a word I will not repeat here.

Her long red fingernails clawed at her chest, trying to remove the cold chocolate ice cream from her boob. She pushed her chair back from the table, knocking over her strawberry milkshake. What was left of her shake poured over the table and down into her luncheon partner's lap.

That woman jumped up, grabbed napkins off the table and dabbed at the pink colored milk and ice cream running over her skirt and down her legs. I recognized her when she gave me her nastiest look. The sunglass woman was Bambi, Mr. B's daughter-in-law.

Why wasn't she somewhere quiet, mourning her loss, or planning Mr. B's funeral?

The toddler stopped screaming and started pointing at Tiffany and laughing.

A waitress dropped a pile of napkins on the table for Bambi, took Tiffany's arm, and headed her toward the lady's room.

Tiffany glared back at me as I stood, holding my empty ice cream cone. "Stay away from Baldacci's, or you'll be sorry!" she managed to spit over her shoulder.

Edna's Diner had become amazingly quiet. Then some of the diners started to laugh quietly. Some not so quietly.

I threaded my way back through the tables, trying to look invisible. It wasn't easy.

When I'd almost made my escape the cashier called out, "Would you like another cone, miss?"

Right then my cheeks were about the color of a Mickey D's sign.

But I had something besides red cheeks to worry about.

Why had Tiffany warned me to stay away from Baldacci's?

Was she just angry about her ruined blouse? Or was something more villainous going on?

One thing I knew for sure. Gramma Rosa owned part of Baldacci's, and no one was going to keep me away from there. I was going to that restaurant any time I wanted to.

Chapter 10

At home I raided the refrigerator and made myself a toasted ham and Swiss with a touch of honey mustard. Mom and Gramma Rosa were still out.

The doorbell rang while I was sweeping up the crumbs.

Two of the black-suited men from Baldacci's back room stood outside. If I hadn't always seen them in those same shiny black suits I might have thought they were in deep mourning for their friend. Those old guys were definitely wardrobe-challenged.

The larger of the men, who almost filled the doorframe by himself, spoke first. "Angelo Serio and Tito Piccolo to call on Mrs. D'Andrea."

The same man I'd heard arguing with Mr. B Wednesday. He didn't mention seeing a skinny girl at the bottom of the stairs next to Mr. B's office that night.

The shorter, skinnier, balder, man, nodded. "Pleased to be here." He stuck out his bony hand. I shook it.

"My grandmother isn't home," I said. "I'll tell her you stopped in." I started to close the door.

Angelo pushed the door open and walked by me. "No problem. We'll wait."

I know a girl alone shouldn't let strangers into the house, but these men weren't exactly strangers. I knew who they were. But they hadn't stopped in for tea and crumpets before. (Not that I had any crumpets on hand to offer them. Tea bags, I had.)

And I couldn't have stopped them from coming in. Angelo Serio alone weighed at least three times more than I did.

They sat on opposite ends of Gramma Rosa's couch, like Alice's friends Tweedledum and Tweedledee.

"Would you like something to drink?" I asked. Maybe this was what guests were like in New Jersey. I was still learning the rules. This was definitely not Seattle.

They looked at each other.

"No, thank you," said Angelo. "But we appreciate your asking. We'll wait."

I sat down on one of the other living room chairs. They were company. I should make conversation. Besides; this was a chance to learn something about my family. Mr. Serio had mentioned the name "Sal" last Wednesday night. Actually, he'd yelled it. "Were you both friends of my grandfather's?" I asked.

Tito Piccolo leaned a little toward me and nodded. "Close friends," he said, meaningfully. "Very close personal friends."

"Then I'm sure my grandmother will be happy to see you," I said. "I never knew my grandfather. What was he like?"

The two men looked at each other. Angelo Serio shifted a little on the couch, as though the cushions under his rear end had rocks in them. He spoke slowly. "Your grandfather was a great man," he said. "He loved his family very much."

He pointed at the wall filled with giant gold framed photographs of Gramma Rosa and Grampa Sal and my mom, when she was young. The three of them, smiling at the Jersey shore. Eating Thanksgiving dinner. In front of a Christmas tree. They looked like a happy family. Not like Grampa Sal had left his family for his daughter's best friend's mother.

The smaller man nodded. "Absolutely. Sal took care of his family and his friends. Always."

I was about to offer the men some leftover desserts when the front door opened and Mom and Gramma Rosa came in. Peppercorns! I'd finally found someone who'd talk to me about Grampa Sal, and they had to come home at that exact moment.

"Mikki!" Mom called from the front hall, "Whose cars are in front of the house?"

Angelo and Tito stood up as she walked in.

"Mom, Mr. Serio and Mr. Piccolo came to see Gramma Rosa," I said.

Mom didn't look happy. "Mother, you have guests. Mikki, excuse yourself and go to your room. You have homework to do."

"It's only Saturday afternoon," I said. I didn't want to miss whatever was going to happen.

"Go to your room, Mikki," said Mom.

"Nice to see you both," I said to the men. I left the living room, but didn't go all the way to my room. I stood around the corner in the hall, hoping to hear what they'd come to talk to Gramma Rosa about.

"Tito, Angelo, sit down," she said brusquely. I heard the wheels of her walker. She was probably going over to her favorite chair, the pink flowered one with the high seat. "Tony's not even under the ground. I didn't expect visitors so soon."

One of the men muttered something. I couldn't understand what he said, but Gramma Rosa's voice came through loud and clear. "Cate, go see to Mikki. Or work on that book of yours. Angelo and Tito and I have some talking to do. They won't be here long."

Whoa! Gramma Rosa was sending Mom to her room the same way Mom sent me. Double peppercorns! I wouldn't be able to hear what they were talking about after all! I headed for my room, fast, so Mom wouldn't know I'd been eavesdropping.

Since we were each in our own rooms, Mom answered the telephone when it rang ten minutes later. She called down the hall, "Mikki, it's for you. Your friend Richard."

(If I had a cell phone, like everyone else in the world my age, I'd have more privacy. But although Gramma Rosa had her own cell, Mom and I used the house phone with the long tangled cord. The same one her family'd had back in the dark ages when she was a teenager.)

I took the phone into my room, closed the door and sat next to the open window so I could see when Angelo and Tito left. Their cars were still parked out front. What were they talking to Gramma Rosa about that was so secret?

"Richard! I thought you had to rake leaves this afternoon."

"I'm taking a break. I've been thinking about Mr. Baldacci. Maybe you're right."

"About telling the police we think he was murdered?" I said.

Now the old guys were leaving, walking down toward the sidewalk. Not looking happy.

"Maybe we could go to the police Monday, after school," Richard said.

"Monday might be too late. We have to talk to the police before the funeral, so they can check the body for poison. Digging the body up after it's been buried would be a lot more complicated." I said.

Angelo stopped twice, turning back to look at our house. What was he looking at?

"OK. I guess that makes sense. But it's already late afternoon. I have to finish raking the yard. Plus, we should give them time to figure out what happened on their own, so maybe we don't have to get involved. How about tomorrow afternoon?"

"Meet me at the library about one o'clock?" I suggested.

"OK," said Richard. "We'll tell our families we're finishing our history papers."

I hung up.

Angelo and Tito were finally getting into their cars. Tito's car was an old black Cadillac. Not one of those cool vintage kinds. Just old, like them. Angelo had a beige mini-van. Whatever they'd talked to Gramma Rosa about, she'd been right. It hadn't taken long.

I spread my history paper notes out on my bed, where I do my best thinking. It was hard to concentrate on the year 1212 when so much was happening in the twenty-first century.

I started making a timeline, the way Mom's detectives do.

6 a.m. Richard and I arrive at Baldacci's restaurant.

Front door locked.

Back door unlocked.

Went in service entrance.

Heard crash from upstairs.

Found Mr. B (skin color red - not pale)

But I'd been awake since before dawn. I fell asleep before I got any further.

Mom didn't even wake me up for dinner.

I didn't hear the sound of the wire cutters on my window screen.

Chapter 11

I was falling.

I couldn't stop. I couldn't wake up.

Everything was in slow motion.

It might be my worst nightmare ever. Maybe I'd fallen down Alice's rabbit hole. I tried to get up, but the air was heavy. Holding me down. I couldn't move.

I gasped, trying to breathe. My head throbbed as if it was going to explode.

I wasn't having a nightmare.

This was worse.

This was real.

I could feel my arms and legs, but I couldn't move them. Something soft was covering my eyes. My mouth felt gummy and smelled ten times worse than morning breath.

When I tried to talk my words came out slurred. "Wayyyyyyyre."

"She's waking up." The voice came from very far away. I concentrated on speaking. My mind was working. My lips weren't.

"So, talk to her. You're the one didn't want to gag her." Tito and Angelo. I was almost positive it was Tito and Angelo. But where was I? Why was I tied up?

"Wayyyyyre Immmm," I tried again, as hard as I could. I sounded like I was under water.

"Hey, Mikki, girl," said the voice that might be Tito's. "You want some water or beer or something?"

"Rosa'll kill you if you give the girl beer," said Angelo. "She's just a kid. You give her beer, that's illegal. You could be arrested for that."

"Right. We got cola, though. Kids like cola, right? Or maybe she's one of those girls who only drink diet stuff? 'Cause we ain't got any diet stuff, do we Angelo?"

"Nah." Angelo sighed. "Not a chance. No diet stuff. We didn't exactly stock up for the occasion. Kid, can we help you sit up?"

I managed to nod.

Big hands picked me up as though I was a doll and leaned me against something. A couch? I raised my hands toward the voices and somehow muttered, "Untie?"

"Go ahead. Untie her," said Tito. "She can drink better that way. She don't know where she is anyhow."

Thick hairy fingers untied my wrists. I shook my arms so the numbness would go away. My wrists tingled as if they were on fire, but the pain was reassuring. It meant feeling had started to come back. Someone put a glass in my right hand. I clasped it with both hands and raised it to my lips. Cola. My lips and throat were parched. I dribbled, but kept gulping, afraid they'd take the glass away. Finally the dryness in my throat and mouth started to disappear.

"Thank you," I rasped, finally. "Now I can talk."

"So, you feeling better?" Tito's voice this time.

"A little." I said. I pulled off the cloth covering my eyes. When the room stopped moving I could see, but everything was out of focus. I had the worst headache I'd ever had, and the bright lights in the room stabbed my eyes.

"Hey! What'd you do? Without the scarf she can see who we are!" said Angelo.

"I knew who you are," I said. "I recognized your voices."

"Smart," said Angelo approvingly. "She's Sal and Rosa's granddaughter. Didn't I tell you she was no bimbo?"

"Too smart for her own good," said Tito. "That's what I told you."

I took a deep breath and started coughing, which made my head hurt more. The spinning room stank of cigarette smoke.

I was sitting on a purple leather couch covered with dark stains. I didn't want to know what the stains were from. A full ashtray overflowed onto the top of a wooden table next to the couch. The circular marks on the tabletop looked like cigarette burns. Red, brown and orange recliners faced an enormous flat screen TV. A pool table filled the space where most people would put a dining table. A pin-ball machine was in one corner. The end of a counter, the only part of the kitchen I could see, was covered with beer and whiskey bottles.

The blue and green quilt Aunt Cierra gave me last Christmas was thrown over the back of the couch. I looked from Angelo to Tito and back to Angelo. "You kidnapped me," I said.

Tito shrugged. "We did what we had to do."

"How?" My ankles were still tied, but I figured I was lucky my hands were free. If the men left me alone I could untie my ankles myself, now that my fingers weren't numb.

"We waited until the lights at your house were off. Then I cut the screen out of your window and crawled in. I put stuff over your face to make sure you'd stay asleep, wrapped you in your quilt so you wouldn't get cold, and handed you out the window to Angelo." Tito paused. "You're heavier than you look."

"I was too big to fit through the window," said Angelo, apologizing for not having broken into my bedroom himself.

"You should lock your windows at night," advised Tito. "Your mother should've taught you better."

"My mother never expected me to be kidnapped," I said, trying hard to stay calm. My head still ached from whatever "stuff" they'd put over my face, although the room was slowing down. I'd never been kidnapped before. What should I do next? What would my kidnappers do? "What time is it?" I didn't see a clock. Ugly purple-flowered drapes covered the three windows in the room.

Angelo looked at his watch. "It is approximately five twenty-three a.m."

"Mom and Gramma Rosa are going to be very worried when they find I'm gone. They'll call the police."

"Nah. They won't," Angelo said confidently. "Rosa knows better than that. We left her a note. We said we'd call her. She'll know you're safe with us."

"I see." I didn't see at all. Did Gramma somehow approve this kidnapping? But I had a feeling that yelling and screaming (which was what I wanted to do, along with crying and asking them to take me home immediately) wouldn't get me anywhere. "So, why? Why did you kidnap me?"

"You was talking on the phone near an open window. We heard it all. You told whoever you was talking to that you was going to the police."

"You said you thought Tony was murdered," said Tito. "Why go to the police?"

"Because I *do* think he was murdered!" I said. "Chief Hunter should find out who killed him!"

Tito and Angelo just shook their heads.

All of a sudden I had a sinking feeling. "That's why you kidnapped me. You. You both. You killed Mr. B, didn't you? You're afraid I'll go to the police and tell them what I know!" I closed my eyes, ready for one of them to confirm my suspicions. "Go ahead. Kill me. It won't help you. The person I was talking to on the telephone knows everything I do. Killing me won't keep the police away."

Tito and Angelo both started laughing. Big, boisterous, rumbling laughs. Laughs that made the pains in my head throb.

"Us? Kill Tony?" Angelo finally managed to say. "Why would we kill Tony? He was one of our best friends."

"Likewise!" agreed Tito. They stopped laughing and looked very serious. "If someone put a hit out on Tony, we should be the ones to find his killer. Then we will revenge his death. The police, they will do nothing!"

"The police," Angelo said, "I spit on them!" And he did. Right on the purple carpet.

"A D'Andrea never goes to the police!" said Tito. "You're young. You're a girl. You're new to Jersey. Maybe you don't know."

"Maybe your grandma, she didn't explain it to you," agreed Angelo. "So we took it into our hands." He looked down at his hands, as though to demonstrate, "To explain what should be done, should you be correct about Tony's demise."

"Should Tony have been snuffed, it had to be by another family," said Tito, very slowly, as though he was explaining the alphabet to a preschooler. "The police do not understand such murders. Angelo and I, on the other hand, have extensive experience dealing with family business. It is to us that such issues should be brought."

"Family business?" Tito said those words the way Tony Soprano would have in *The Sopranos.* Mom would not be happy about this conversation. I wasn't sure about everything the men were saying but I was sure about a few basics. I was not in a TV show or movie. And Tito and Angelo were taking me seriously. If I said Mr. B was murdered, they were willing to listen. "What family would be interested in getting rid of Mr. B?" I asked. I hoped I didn't sound as dumb as I felt.

"We would have to listen around, you understand," said Tito. "To be sure."

"True," said Angelo. "But the family most likely would be the Morellis. The Morellis and the D'Andreas have always been in competition with each other."

"What you say is indeed factual," said Tito. "Although that competition has not resulted in violence for some years. And Tony always made sure he was never in a position for such a thing as snuffing to happen to him."

"Absolutely," Angelo acknowledged. "Still, the Morelli family is the obvious place to begin. Plus, I believe there is a local connection. Remember Louie Morelli, from the old days?"

He turned to Tito. "His son Bobby now lives in Edgewood. I have personally observed him eating pizza at Baldacci's on more than one occasion."

At that point the throbbing in my head got seriously worse. "Bobby Morelli?" I asked. "You mean Robert Morelli? You think he killed Mr. B?"

"I believe Robert is the formal name of that Morelli," said Angelo. "So. You know this man?"

I'd suspected these guys were a little over the edge. Now I knew they were seriously messed up. "Robert Morelli's my history teacher."

Chapter 12

Mr. Morelli wasn't my favorite teacher. But no way was he a killer.

Somewhere in this place they'd brought me to there must be a rocker, because Angelo and Tito were definitely off it.

"He must not be in the same Morelli family you're thinking of," I said, looking from one of the men to the other. "The Robert Morelli I know teaches ninth grade history. He's boring. A geek. He wears glasses and loves stuff that happened centuries ago."

"He could be undercover," explained Tito. "Family members may have jobs not directly related to family business."

"Or the girl could be correct," allowed Angelo. "Young people today cannot always be trusted to carry on family traditions."

I'd been listening to Mom plot her mysteries since before I could read *Harriet the Spy* or Nancy Drew. I knew the ropes. Sure, some people were killed by street violence. But most murders involved reason and logic, or at least what passed for logic in the minds of the nutcases doing the killing. There had to be motive, opportunity and means. I didn't see any of those connecting Mr. Morelli to Mr. B.

"Why would someone in the Morelli family want to kill Mr. B?" I asked, trying to understand. "You have to have a reason to kill someone. A motive."

"The girl is intelligent," Tito pointed out to Angelo. I started to nod, when he added, "But she is not yet well informed." He turned to me. "In many murders, what you say is true. Motive is an important thing."

"That is what the police will tell you," said Angelo. "I spit on the police." And so he did. Again. Spitting was clearly one of Angelo's punctuation marks. "With family killings, however, sometimes motives are not so clear."

Again with these mysterious "family killings."

"Killings might be for matters known only within the family, or within the context of family business." Tito smiled broadly and spread his arms out as though his explanation encompassed the world. "Or to avenge a past event."

What he said made no sense to me. Of course, the continued pounding inside my head wasn't helping me focus.

"Gramma Rosa said Mr. B's only family was his son and his son's wife," I said.

The two men looked at each other. "True, once again," said Tito. "But of no importance."

"So? What's the family problem between Mr. B and Mr. Morelli?" I asked.

"Never has there been a direct problem between Tony and the Morellis," explained Tito, very slowly this time.

"And without doubt it has been many years since there have been feuds between the Morellis and the D'Andreas," Angelo admitted.

"Still, the possibility cannot be ruled out without investigation," said Tito. "Seeing as Tony was a close friend of the D'Andreas."

"Agreed." Angelo smiled widely. "And such an investigation we will be happy to take on."

I gave up. I didn't understand what Tito and Angelo were talking about, and clearly there was no talking them out of whatever it was they were going to do. What harm would it be to have them investigate? I reached down and untied the rope around my ankles. Lowering my head made the throbbing in my head worse.

"Can you take me home now?" I asked. "Please?"

The men looked at each other and then back at me. "You understand, now, why you cannot go to the police."

I had no clue. But I really, really, wanted to get out of there.

"I won't go to the police," I agreed.

I didn't promise Richard wouldn't go to the police. Or that I didn't think these men were basically out of their minds. That I thought their combined IQs were about two points short of a pint of Italian olive oil. The expensive kind.

"And we will take over the investigation of the Morelli Family, on Tony's behalf," said Angelo.

"Agreed," said Tito. "You also agree, Mikki?"

I nodded. I wasn't exactly sure what I was agreeing to. But agreeing seemed smart under the circumstances. To quote them: I was no bimbo.

Angelo hoisted me back through my window a little before seven o'clock Sunday morning. He handed my quilt in after me. I would much rather have gone in through the front door, but I didn't have my key.

I waved goodbye as they drove off. Then I closed the window, locked it, and tore up the note they'd left on my bed for Gramma Rosa.

I hoped no one would notice the neatly cut screen lying on the ground underneath my window.

I pushed my history paper notes aside, took two Tylenols for my headache, and lay down on my bed. Maybe I could get a few minutes of sleep before Mom and Gramma Rosa were ready for breakfast.

At least I was home. Would Mr. Morelli accept kidnapping as a reason for not getting my history paper in on time? I had a feeling it wasn't on the usual list of acceptable excuses.

Chapter 13

I'm not the kind of girl who'd let a little thing like being kidnapped interfere with Sunday breakfast.

Two hours later I splashed water on my face, brushed my teeth, and headed to the kitchen.

One good thing about Jersey is that you can get really good New York City bagels there. (I haven't gotten to New York City itself yet, but it's definitely high on my "want to do" list.) My favorite bagel flavor is the "everything": deep taste of kosher salt, dried onion, garlic, poppy seeds, and whatever else the baker chooses to throw into his herb mix. An East Coast classic.

Mom had left to get the Sunday newspapers and pick up bagels, lox, and cream cheese and I was pouring myself a glass of OJ when the doorbell rang. Anyone would think we were used to having a lot of company.

"Good morning, Mikki Norden."

Peppercorns. Standing outside our front door was Chief Hunter, Edgewood's own protector-of-the-innocent. The very person I had recently promised two particular gentlemen I wouldn't speak to.

"I'd like to see your mother." He looked over my head as though Mom might appear at any moment.

"She's out," I said.

He looked disappointed. What had Mom done to have a cop looking for her?

"Then could I speak with your grandmother?"

I suddenly felt very protective of Gramma Rosa. Why did Chief Hunter need to see anyone in my family?

One thing I'd learned from Tito and Angelo: "family" was a strong word. You loved and protected your family no matter what. "She's not up yet."

"I see," he said.

We stood, staring at each other. "Her arthritis is bad. It takes her a long time to get up and dressed in the morning," I said, in case he planned to come in and sit on the couch and wait, the way Tito and Angelo had the day before. Then I couldn't resist adding, "Do you have Mr. Baldacci's autopsy results yet?" I hadn't promised Tito and Angelo I wouldn't ask about the autopsy.

Chief Hunter looked surprised. "There's not going to be an autopsy, Mikki. No need."

"But if there's no autopsy, how will you know whether or not he was murdered?" Unbelievable!

"Mr. Baldacci was almost seventy years old. He had a history of heart problems. His doctor signed the death certificate. There's no reason to think he was murdered." Chief Hunter talked slowly, as if he was explaining that my goldfish had died. I was getting way tired of people acting as if I didn't understand what was going one. "People die, Mikki. Most of the time no one's at fault. It's the way life is." Then he paused. "Unless you know something else. Have you heard anything you need to tell me?"

I was dying to tell him. I was not dying to be kidnapped again.

I shook my head.

Chief Hunter turned to leave, but hesitated. "He was your friend, Mikki, and it's sad he died. Accept it. Put it behind you. And don't forget to tell your mother and grandmother I stopped in."

I watched him walk down the path and get in his car. I wanted to run up to him and shake him. I wanted to say, "You're wrong!" and tell him every bit of evidence Richard and I'd found.

But I didn't.

I was a D'Andrea, and D'Andreas don't talk to the police.

That rule was definitely limiting my options.

I was sure someone had killed Mr. B.

Now I was sure the police weren't going to investigate.

I was going to have to do it myself.

I didn't trust my new BFFs Tito and Angelo to get the job done.

Chapter 14

Mom got home a few minutes after Chief Hunter left.

Like every Sunday, she put the newspapers and the bagels down on the coffee table and poured herself a cup of coffee. Then she went to help Gramma Rosa get dressed.

She'd bought garlic and onion bagels, and cream cheese. Not my favs, but good. No lox this week. Some people like butter on their bagels, but for me, a bagel absolutely requires cream cheese. I sliced a garlic one and started it toasting. Then I chopped two scallions and mixed them and ground black pepper into the cream cheese. Nothing like cream cheese with scallions on a warm toasted bagel to begin a Sunday morning.

After a few bites I picked up the *Star Ledger*, and started looking through the obituaries.

"Anthony Francis Baldacci" was listed. He'd been born in Newark sixty-eight years ago and died at his restaurant in Edgewood, which he'd owned for thirty-four years. His wife predeceased him. He was survived by his son, Lucas Anthony Baldacci of New York City, and Lucas' wife, Bambi. Services would be held at St. Joseph's Church in Edgewood on Monday afternoon at two o'clock.

Nothing about what a wonderful man he was, or how caring he was, or how he laughed at bad jokes, or about his super special pizza sauce, or how he would be missed. An obituary is like the front and back covers of a book without pages between them. You knew when someone's life began and when it ended, but there weren't many details about what happened in between.

"Mr. B's obituary is in the paper. His funeral's going to be at St. Joseph's on Monday afternoon," I called down the hall.

"We'll all go, of course," said Gramma Rosa, appearing in the doorway. "Let me see that, Mikki." I folded the *Ledger* to the obituary page and put it on the table next to her chair.

"Chief Hunter from the police department was here a little while ago, Gramma. He wanted to talk to you and Mom. I told him you weren't up yet."

Gramma Rosa touched my arm lightly. "Thank you, Mikki. Please don't mention that to your mother. I'm not sure she's ready to talk to him. It might upset her. I'll call him later."

I wondered how upset Mom would be if I casually mentioned that, by the way, I'd been kidnapped the night before. I glanced at my wrists and pulled down the sleeves of my sweatshirt so they covered the rope burns. My head still ached, but sleep and Tylenol had helped. The bagel hadn't hurt either.

I heated water for Gramma Rosa's tea.

"Mikki doesn't have to go to the funeral, Mother. She has school tomorrow." Mom sat down on the couch with her cup of coffee and started layering my cream cheese and scallion mixture onto her bagel.

"You can write a note to excuse me," I called in to the living room. "I could leave after English class. I wouldn't miss anything except art." And history, I added silently to myself. Mr. Morelli's history class. Mr. Morelli of the dangerous Morelli family.

Attending Mr. B's funeral was more important than missing one history class. I'd hand in my paper before I left school.

"Tony was a family friend. Mikki should be there. The school must excuse students for funerals," said Gramma Rosa. "We'll pick you up at school, Mikki."

Yes! In this house Gramma Rosa ruled.

I put her tea on the table next to her.

I definitely wanted to be at that funeral. I wanted to see who'd show up. In books and movies the murderer often went to the funerals of his victim.

Mom sighed. "I'll write you a note. But you'll have to find something decent to wear. Not jeans. Do you have a dark skirt and top?" Questions regarding proper clothing usually didn't concern Mom. But, then, we hadn't attended a lot of funerals.

"I'll look." I fled to my bedroom. I didn't think I had the kind of clothes Mom was thinking about, but I really needed to talk to someone. I couldn't tell Mom or Gramma Rosa I'd been kidnapped. They were upset enough that Mr. B had died. And of course even if I'd wanted to talk to Dad, he was unreachable. Right now he was probably having brunch with Sung Ja and her mom. His new family.

Families were supposed to be forever. The people you could go to for help no matter what happened. Or was that just in books?

But if I couldn't talk to anyone in my family, I could talk to Richard. We'd planned to meet at the library at one o'clock. I suddenly had a horrible feeling that he wouldn't be there.

If only I had a cell and could text. No one called their friends any more. They especially didn't call someone's house where anyone could answer. But I looked up Richard's home telephone number on Mom's computer anyway.

Sure enough, his father picked up the phone. "Mikki Norden? I'll see if Richard is available." I could hear his father yell, "Richard! A girl named Mikki is on the telephone for you. Do you want to talk to her?"

The next voice I heard was Richard's.

"Mikki? What is it?"

"I really need to talk to you. It's important. You *are* going to meet me at the library this afternoon, right?"

"We said at one o'clock." Richard lowered his voice. "Is everything all right?"

"Weird things are happening. Can you be there a little earlier than one?"

"Twelve-thirty? The library doesn't open until noon on Sundays."

"See you at twelve-thirty."

Chapter 15

I got to the library at twelve-fifteen. Richard wasn't there so I headed for the computer room. I'd gotten a start on my history paper before he pulled a chair up beside mine. "So, what's happening?" He peeked over at the screen. "You haven't finished your paper?"

"You have?"

"Last night. I have a computer at home. You don't?"

"Mom and I share one. But she's always writing a critical scene or counting red herrings. I hardly ever get a chance to use it."

"Red herrings?" Richard looked at me strangely. Sometimes I forget Mom and I live in sort of another world.

"Red herrings. Fake clues in mysteries that an author puts in to mislead the reader."

"Oh. I figured they were something else you were cooking."

I tried not to laugh. Why *did* they call those false clues red herrings anyway? I closed the file and pulled my thumb drive out of the computer.

Richard nodded. "So?"

I hardly knew where to start. "They didn't do an autopsy on Mr. Baldacci."

He frowned. "How do you know that?"

"Chief Hunter came to my house this morning. I asked him."

"He came to your house?" Richard looked disbelieving. "Why?"

"He wanted to talk to my mom. She was out. Then he asked for my grandmother. She wasn't even up yet."

"Why would he want to talk to your mother or grandmother?" asked Richard.

"I don't know. Maybe it has something to do with Baldacci's restaurant. Remember? My grandmother's a silent partner there."

"Is that the 'weird stuff' you said was happening?" Richard asked.

"That, plus a couple of Mr. B's friends stopped in to see Gramma Rosa late yesterday. She wanted to talk with them privately."

"So. Parents and grandparents need their privacy, same as kids do. What's strange about that?" asked Richard.

Would Richard even believe my story? "Later last night those same two guys broke into my room and drugged and kidnapped me."

"What?" Richard looked as though I'd just told him I'd had breakfast with the white rabbit. He actually moved his chair back a little. "So how come you're here now?"

"Because after I promised them I wouldn't go to the police about Mr. B's murder they took me home. Even Mom and Gramma don't know what happened." I held out my arms and pulled up the sleeves of my sweatshirt. The rope burns on my wrists were pretty obvious. "I didn't do that to myself. There are marks on my ankles, too."

Richard looked at my wrists, and then at me. "Tell me what happened."

I did.

"They really think Mr. Morelli might have killed Mr. Baldacci?" said Richard.

"That's what they said," I told him. "That part was pretty strange."

"*That part*?" said Richard. "Your whole story sounds off the wall to me. Except for two things."

"Two things?"

"First, your rope burns. I don't think you're strange enough to do that to yourself."

"Thank *you*!" I said, rubbing one of my wrists. It stung.

"And, second, there's your family."

"What's this thing everyone in New Jersey has about family?" I asked. "Everyone talks about family – especially *my* family – as though it's a code word or something!"

Richard took a deep breath. "Mikki, when you lived in Seattle, did your mom ever talk to you about growing up in Edgewood? About her family?"

"She said she didn't get along with her dad. She left Edgewood when she went to college and hasn't been home again until now."

Richard looked embarrassed. "I kind of thought that was true. I mean, I hardly know you. But my dad … after you called he asked who you were. He's really big on knowing who I hang out with and all. I told him your name and where you lived."

"Yeah?" I asked. What was this thing everyone had about where I lived? Was the house haunted or something?

"He wasn't too happy about my meeting you."

"He doesn't even know me!" I said.

"He knows your family." Richard looked as though he really wanted to leave the library right then. "I mean he knows *about* your family. A lot of people know about your family. I told him you weren't like them. He still wasn't too happy when I said we were friends."

We were friends! I liked that. I had a friend in Edgewood. "What about my family?" I was getting impatient. "Gramma Rosa's a little eccentric, but she's just an old lady who uses a pink walker."

"Your grandfather was Sal D'Andrea," said Richard, blurting it out as though it was a major confession.

"So?" I said. That wasn't news. I knew my grandfather's name.

"He was killed in prison two years ago."

That *was* news. I suddenly felt a deep hole somewhere near my stomach. Had part of me already guessed something like that? Maybe I hadn't wanted to connect the dots. "What was he in prison for?"

"You didn't know then," Richard said. "I didn't think you did." He looked around, as though he was deciding whether to run or to stay. He stayed. "He was convicted of a whole lot of stuff. Racketeering, mostly. Murders, too. Your grandfather was head of one of the biggest organized crime families in Jersey. He'd been in jail for almost fifteen years. A lot of people around here remember." He grimaced a little. "My dad sure does."

"My grandfather was a gangster? Like in *The Sopranos*?" Richard's words were hitting my brain as though they were in slow motion.

"According to my dad, he was the boss."

"Whatever he did, he went to jail for it before you and I were born. Your dad isn't happy you're talking to me because of something my grandfather did before we were even born?" Now I was connecting. Now I was getting angry. "That's crazy!"

"Sort of," Richard admitted. "But Dad said families like yours, the kind involved with organized crime, stay involved with crime."

"So? You think crime is in my genes? Maybe you think *I* killed Mr. B?" My voice got louder than it should.

A librarian across the room frowned at me.

I lowered my voice. "Or maybe my grandmother did it. You've met her. She looked pretty dangerous, didn't she? You think that pink walker of hers could be a lethal weapon?"

"Hey, Mikki! Calm down," Richard backed up a bit. "I'm on your side. I'm here, aren't I? But your family's history could explain why Chief Hunter went to your house this morning."

I tried to think rationally. "I suppose."

"And … your Mr. Baldacci was Italian, like your grandfather. Maybe he was involved with your grandfather's … business."

"Not Mr. B! He couldn't have been!" I'd never met my grandfather. But I'd known Mr. B. He was no criminal. He was a chef, like me! Or, like I was going to be. Chefs weren't gangsters. Handy with knives, maybe. But gangsters? No way.

"And those other men who came to see your grandmother. You said they were a little strange. Maybe they worked for your grandfather."

"They did," I admitted. "And Angelo Serio, the big one? I heard him arguing with Mr. B last Wednesday night, when I went to the restaurant to borrow the mascarpone. He was asking for money."

"Did Mr. Baldacci give it to him?"

"He said he didn't have it. Angelo was pretty angry." With everything else that had happened I'd almost forgotten what I'd heard that night.

"That sounds suspicious," said Richard. "If Mr. Baldacci wouldn't give him money, couldn't that be a motive to kill him?"

"Maybe." But I remembered how Tito and Angelo had acted when they'd thought about Mr. B being murdered. They hadn't acted guilty. They'd been angry. "But Mr. B was his friend. If Angelo killed his friend, he'd never get any money from him." I shook my head. "I don't think it was him. He was upset, but I don't think he killed anyone."

Richard looked doubtful. "But he's a gangster. Gangsters kill people!"

My head was whirring. Why hadn't Mom warned me about this? She must have known I'd find out someday.

Here I'd thought I was just a regular kid. A regular kid who liked to make cream puffs and lasagna noodles from scratch and dreamed of studying in Paris and owning her own restaurant and writing cookbooks.

Instead I find out I'm living in some *Godfather* or *Sopranos* movie. Only it's not a movie. It's my own family.

I even got kidnapped by two bozos who knew more about my family than I did. Tito and Angelo had convinced me they had nothing to do with Mr. B's death. But if they were gangsters, could I really believe them? Who could I believe?

Were Mom and Gramma Rosa involved with all this stuff too? Who was I supposed to trust?

"I have to go home now," I said. "I have to talk to my family."

"Be careful," said Richard. "Now that you know who they are, they might be dangerous, Mikki."

Peppercorns.

That was just what I needed to hear.

Chapter 16

I'd gotten all the way home before I realized Richard and I hadn't even talked about going to the police about Mr. B's smelling of almonds. I'd planned to convince Richard to go alone so I wouldn't break my word to Tito and Angelo. (I was beginning to think of them as Tweedledee and Tweedledumb.)

Somehow talking to the police didn't seem as important anymore. Not if everyone in Edgewood believed Gramma Rosa and Mom and I were criminals. Maybe even serial killers.

Maybe they thought my wanting to be a chef was a charade. Maybe I was really planning to capture Edgewood's children and bake them up in my oven, like the witch in *Hansel and Gretel.*

Families might push (or kick) you in certain directions. But that didn't mean you'd follow that road. Okay; maybe Grampa Sal had been a little shady. Maybe more than a little. But I was Mikki Norden, like Mom said. I wasn't Sal D'Andrea. I sure wasn't planning to pattern my life on his.

Mom was his daughter, and she wasn't dangerous. At least not to anyone who wasn't fictional. After all, she'd left Edgewood years ago because she and her dad hadn't gotten along. Right now that sounded like the smartest move I'd heard about all day. And how could Gramma Rosa be involved with anything sinister? She was old. She was sad because Mr. B had died. How could I ask her what being a D'Andrea meant?

I needed Mom or Gramma to tell me about the family themselves, not learn about it on-line. Right now I was sure everyone in New Jersey was crazy *except* my family.

And I had questions. Like, why did Gramma Rosa take so many telephone calls privately in her room?

And what about Angelo and Tito, who said they were friends of my grandfather's (now not a good sign) but were also friends of Mr. B's? They hadn't really hurt me, but they had kidnapped me.

Friends don't kidnap other friends, do they?

I was from Seattle. Maybe in New Jersey they did.

My mind zoomed in all sorts of directions. One direction included my homework that was due Monday morning. It had to be done, too. I could depend on school to be normal. (Except maybe for Mr. Morelli, my killer history teacher.)

I should talk with Mom.

She'd grown up here. In the very same house where we lived now. She'd survived. She'd understand. She might even find some way to move us back to Seattle, where people were normal. Maybe we could take Gramma Rosa with us. People used walkers in Seattle, too.

I walked faster toward home. That's what I'd do. I'd talk to Mom.

Usually talking to her wasn't a problem. True, sometimes I had to pull her away from a murder scene or police chase or a fight to the death. And sometimes she didn't listen as closely as I'd like. But I could count on her almost always being available.

Of course, because today I needed to be reassured that everything was normal, nothing was as usual.

The good news was I could use Mom's computer to finish my history paper. Mom and Gramma Rosa spent most of the afternoon on the telephone to people I didn't know, talking about Mr. B's funeral. For dinner we ordered pizza from a chain store in the next town. That was a sure sign Mom and Gramma Rosa were upset. They didn't even want me in the kitchen. They wanted me in another room, out of the way.

(The sauce on the delivered pizza was flat and gummy and sweet; not even close to Baldacci's tomato sauce in texture or flavor. Yuck.)

I managed (wide margins) to stretch my history paper to five pages. The only other homework I had was two pages of algebra. Algebra's a lot easier than history or English. In algebra there's only one right answer. You either get something right or you don't.

"Mikki, have you found something to wear to the funeral tomorrow?" Mom asked about nine o'clock that night.

The only dress in my closet was a red flowered sundress a friend of Mom's sent me from Florida a couple of years ago. And it didn't fit. Why do people have to wear dark, boring clothes to a funeral? Mr. B wouldn't have cared what I looked like.

I'd covered my bed with every piece of clothing I owned by the time Mom came to inspect. "Found anything?"

"Navy two piece bathing suit?" I asked, holding the bottom half up.

She sighed. "I was afraid of that. Hold on." In a couple of minutes she was back. "See if this works." She held out a skirt of hers. Boring. Navy blue.

"You're taller than I am," I said, eying it. I'm not picky about clothes. But that skirt was definitely not cool.

"Not taller by much," she said. "And the waist is too small for me. Try."

It sort of fit. And, okay. The situation was desperate. I really wanted to go to that funeral. "It's loose," I said, putting both my fists between my skin and the waistband of the skirt. "And it hangs low." The waist was about three inches below my belly button.

"Hmmm. Have you got a white tee shirt?" Mom asked. "No words or pictures. Just white."

I dug through the pile on my bed and came up with one from a couple of years ago. Sung Ja and I had spent two fun days tie-dying tee shirts (and ourselves.) This shirt had escaped.

"Put it on over the skirt so it covers the waist."

We both looked.

"Not bad." Mom looked me over. "Not perfect, but not bad. Pin the waist of the skirt so it fits tighter. You only have to wear it at the funeral. We'll be sitting down most of the time."

I looked in the mirror. "I can live with it for the funeral. But I can't be seen wearing it to school. Can I wear the tee shirt over jeans in the morning and then change into the skirt in the car on the way to the funeral?"

Mom put up her hand for a high-five. "Done. Now put the rest of those clothes away and get ready for bed. I still have to decide what I'm going to wear tomorrow."

I wanted to ask Mom about our family, and what people really thought about us, and about Tito and Angelo, but she was so involved with the funeral, and clothes, and Gramma Rosa, there wasn't a minute when I could talk to her alone.

My questions would have to wait until after the funeral.

Chapter 17

When we got to the church it was clear Gramma Rosa was the most properly clad of the three of us. At her age, she'd probably been to more funerals than Mom or me. She wore a navy blue dress and matching jacket and a three-strand pearl necklace. Other Edgewood women had pulled similar outfits out of their closets. Funerals must be part of the New Jersey social scene.

All the handicapped parking spaces at the church were filled by the time we got there, so Mom let Gramma Rosa and I out near the church door. That way Gramma wouldn't have to walk too far.

While Mom parked at the far end of the parking lot we watched as car after car pulled up and a crew videotaped each mourner. The hostess at Baldacci's, Tiffany, seemed to be telling the crew what to do. Most people took one look at the camera and ducked inside the church, away from the camera lens, as fast as possible. A lot of them wore big hats that covered their faces.

"Why are they filming?" I asked Gramma. "Is the funeral going to be on the news?"

"Some people have no sense of propriety," she said, pulling her own hat down to hide her face and looking the other way.

"The police are here, too." I pointed at the cop cars parked across the street from the church.

"No reason they should be here except to direct traffic," she said. "They know that." She tapped her walker impatiently on the uneven sidewalk while we waited for Mom to come back.

"We'll sit up front, where the action is," she announced as soon as we entered the church. She didn't whisper. A couple of people already sitting in the sanctuary turned around to stare.

"Mother, we aren't members of this parish. Maybe we should sit in the back," Mom said softly.

"Phooey. We were close friends of Tony's. He's up front, and that's where we should be." Gramma Rosa wheeled her walker past Mom and I and down the main aisle.

Large flower arrangements were lined up across the front of the church. Right in the middle was a casket. The lid was open.

Mr. B was in there.

I'd already seen him at the restaurant. I wanted to remember him, smiling and laughing. I didn't want to see him in a box.

I didn't move.

Gramma Rosa was moving her walker right along. She was getting further down the aisle by the minute.

"Come on, Mikki. We need to stay with Gramma. She might fall," Mom said, tugging on my arm.

I walked after Mom, trying to look at Gramma Rosa and not past her at Mr. B. It was hard. It's almost impossible to stop yourself from seeing something unless you close your eyes, and I couldn't do that and walk down the aisle.

We were a parade. Gramma Rosa, thumping her pink walker down that center aisle, passing rows of people saying their rosaries or checking to see who else was coming in. Followed by Mom, followed by me. Gramma Rosa made it almost all the way to the front when a tall man in a suit and tie stopped her. He whispered something.

"A *close* friend," she said loudly.

He showed us to the second row, right in back of a pew marked "reserved for family."

Mom went into the row first, and then I did, and then Gramma Rosa, so she and her walker could be on the aisle.

As soon as the usher left to seat someone else she popped up again. "I'm going to say goodbye to Tony," she said. She took off, heading straight for the coffin.

Mom nudged me. Hard. I didn't have a choice. I went after Gramma, hoping it looked as though I was helping my dear, sweet grandmother, and not trying my darndest to get her back to her seat.

I held her arm and whispered, "Gramma Rosa. Come back and sit down."

"I'm here to say goodbye to Tony, and that's what I plan to do," she whispered back. Then she winked at me. I gave up. There was nothing I could do but make sure she did what she wanted to do as quickly as possible. I glanced back at the church. People were definitely watching us. We were at the front of the church. It was show time, and we were the show.

My cheeks were getting redder every moment.

The church was filling rapidly. Most of the kitchen staff and waitresses who'd worked at Baldacci's Restaurant were sitting in the back, where I wished I was. I glanced again. A lot of men in one section were wearing the same style black suit and tie Angelo and Tito had worn Saturday. In fact, I was pretty sure Angelo and Tito were there, too.

I wanted to see exactly who was in the church, in case the murderer was there, but, instead, I had to make sure Gramma Rosa didn't lose her balance. I suspected she'd had at least a glass or three of Chianti to fortify herself before the funeral.

The coffin was surrounded by large wreaths of white chrysanthemums. The smell was overpoweringly sweet. I crinkled my nose, trying hard not to sneeze.

Gramma Rosa bent over the coffin. Mr. B's face was pale with makeup except where he was painted with blusher and lipstick. He didn't look at all like my Mr. B. "Goodbye, Tony. Say hello to my dear Sal for me. I'll be seeing you both soon."

As I listened to her deliver her message I suddenly felt a sharp pain near my stomach. The safety pin I'd used to tighten Mom's navy blue skirt had opened. The skirt started to slide. Down. Fast. I grabbed for it, but right then Gramma Rosa tried to turn her walker around to return to her seat. She slipped. I grabbed her arm to steady her.

And my skirt slid. Down. Further. All the way down.

Gramma Rosa didn't notice. She was balancing on her walker with one hand and dabbing her eyes with an embroidered lace handkerchief with her other.

Everyone else in the church saw clearly.

I was standing there in front of God and everyone in my white tee shirt and my red cotton underpants, my mother's blue skirt bunched around my ankles. Giggling and guffaws erupted from far corners of the church.

I felt my face turn from pink to scarlet. But what was I supposed to do? Dump Gramma Rosa? I tried to be cool. I stepped out of the skirt, held onto Gramma with one hand, and with the other reached down and picked up the skirt.

And looked straight up into the face of Mr. Baldacci's son, Luc, and his wife, Bambi, as the usher conducted them down the aisle to their "reserved for family" seats.

Somehow I got Gramma Rosa and her walker around them and into our row, and then was able to pull my skirt up and wriggle into it. Mom, her face almost as red as mine, shook her head in sympathy and dug in her pocketbook for another safety pin.

I don't remember much of the actual service. I just remember thinking this would be a perfect time to move back to Seattle. Immediately and permanently.

Chapter 18

Mom put a firm hand over Gramma Rosa's to ensure that we were among the last to leave the church and say our "so very sorry for your loss"es to Mr. B's son and his wife. (Bambi Baldacci was not wearing her dark sunglasses today.)

So Gramma Rosa and I were waiting for Mom to get our car when Mr. B's son and daughter-in-law walked out of St. Joseph's.

"We need to talk, Mrs. D'Andrea," said Luc. "The night before he died my father told me about the partnership you and he formed to expand his restaurant."

"*Our* restaurant," said Gramma Rosa, calmly. "I was a silent partner, but a partner, just the same. He wanted to expand the restaurant. I provided the funding for him to do that."

"I understand," said Luc. "But now the situation has changed. The expansion won't be going forward."

Bambi smiled very sweetly. "We want to keep the restaurant just the way it's always been, don't we, dear?" she said.

"That's your decision," Gramma Rosa said, equally sweetly. "But contracts have been signed with the architect and contractors. Deposits have been made. I've invested a sizeable amount of money in this project. I've already talked with my lawyer. If you'd like to buy out my share I expect to be reimbursed for every penny I've invested, and, of course, paid for the emotional stress the disappointment of cancelling such a project would be for someone of my advanced age." Gramma Rosa reached into her large black purse and handed Luc Baldacci a card. "Here's my lawyer's name. He's expecting to hear from you." She turned to me. "Mikki, would you help me to our car? I'm feeling a bit faint. It's been an exhausting day."

I took Gramma Rosa's arm. Bambi Baldacci looked furious; Luc Baldacci looked stricken. Clearly neither of them knew my grandmother.

At home, Gramma Rosa and Mom and I sat in the living room. Gramma didn't seem at all faint. She asked me to get her a cup of strong tea, with cognac.

While the water was heating I made cocoa for myself, and cut us all slices of cinnamon bread I'd made and frozen a couple of weeks ago. Gramma Rosa needed to eat something with her tea, and I could use a snack.

Finally, food and drink taken care of, I couldn't hold my questions in any longer.

"Why didn't one of you tell me Grampa was a gangster? Everyone in town seems to know except me. And were all those men in black suits at the funeral gangsters too? And what about Mr. B? Was he involved with organized crime? Please be honest with me! I need to know what everyone else in town knows."

Mom and Gramma Rosa looked at each other. Gramma Rosa took a long sip of tea.

Then Mom blurted, "See, Mother? This is why I wanted to raise my daughter in Seattle, far away from everything in New Jersey. I didn't want her to grow up the way I did, with bodyguards following me around. Never knowing when someone called Uncle Freddy would disappear and turn up in the Meadowlands, shot in the head!"

"You're exaggerating, Cate. Uncle Freddy drowned in the

Hudson River," said Gramma Rosa calmly, putting down her tea cup. "Your grampa was not exactly a gangster, Mikki. He was more an organizer. He protected people who ran small businesses. He made sure nothing bad happened to them, like sudden fires, or robberies. Not to say sometimes he and the people he worked with didn't have troubles."

"Like with the police?" I asked.

"The police, sometimes. Sometimes other people in the same business. To be truthful, it wasn't a very polite business. But your grandfather loved your mother and me, and he would have loved you, too, if he'd known you. And he took good care of the people who worked with him."

"People like Angelo Serio and Tito Piccolo?" I asked.

"They were both close to him." Gramma nodded.

"And Mr. B?" I asked.

"Tony?" Gramma Rosa said. "Tony was different. A friend, yes. But not a business friend. A personal friend. Tony was from the old neighborhood, where a lot of us grew up. He went into the restaurant business; not the same business as my Sal. When he moved to Edgewood and opened his restaurant here he made a place where Sal and his friends could meet, and eat and drink. No problems for him; no problems for them."

"So if he wasn't a gangster, why were the police at the funeral today? And who were the people with cameras?" I was tired of half answers.

"The police were there because of Tony's friends. Some of them … well, a few may still be active in the business. Police come to funerals when someone connected dies. It's kind of a New Jersey tradition. And sometimes the police do help with parking, like I told you." Gramma Rosa smiled. I believed she was telling me the whole truth. Her whole truth.

Mom sighed. "Mother. You told Mikki the police were there to help with the parking?"

"They might be. You never know!" said Gramma Rosa. She'd almost finished her cup of tea-with-cognac.

"And the people with cameras?" I asked again.

"That's another story. Those are sleazy friends of Bambi Baldacci's."

"Mr. Baldacci's daughter-in-law?" What did she have to do with all this?

"That woman is a pain in the you-know-what. She knows someone who produces those television programs where they follow real people around and the real people act crazy. What do you call that?"

"A reality show?" I guessed.

"That's it! Reality show. Well, she and her friend have been trying to sell the idea of filming one of those awful shows about the people in Tony's restaurant. Real people, like my dear Sal used to be, bless his soul."

"She wanted to have a reality show about gangsters?" I said, beginning to get the picture. A strange and cloudy picture, but a picture. "Like the *Sopranos*, only with real people?"

"So she thought," said Gramma Rosa. "Only, Tito and Angelo, and the others, *Sopranos* actors, they're not. Not even to mention that nothing of interest is happening at Baldacci's today. Television would only bring back bad memories. Tony, he told her she was nuts. But she liked the way the restaurant looked, and the idea of the back room, and she kept telling him this television show of hers would make Baldacci's famous."

"But it is famous! Restaurant reviewers made it famous! His pizza sauce made it famous!" I said. "That's the way a restaurant should be famous."

"Exactly. Which is why Tony kept saying 'no' to that Bambi. She even had the nerve once to ask me to influence him. Can you believe?" Gramma Rosa stared into her tea cup with some surprise. It was empty. She handed it to me.

"So the cameras today?" I asked, taking the cup and heading to the kitchen.

"I think they're part of her plan. She wants pictures of people connected with the restaurant. Especially since now she and her husband are going to own it."

"But you own part of it," I reminded her.

"Ah, yes. They can't own the whole restaurant without buying me out first," Gramma Rosa said. "And your grandmother is no stupid woman. If they want Tony's restaurant, they will pay through the nose." She smiled very sweetly. "Mikki, dear, you're getting me another cup of tea, aren't you? This time, a little heavier on the cognac, please. I'm in mourning."

Chapter 19

After hearing that, I needed to think. To relax. To cook.

We each had our own way of calming down. Gramma Rosa was on her third tea-plus-cognac. Mom had retreated to her bedroom and was keyboarding like mad. (Either she'd figured out a new way to kill Frankie, or she'd started a whole new book. Her autobiography might be interesting.)

I was going to make dinner.

I turned the oven on high and got out eggs and flour and onions for my favorite popovers. While they were rising in the oven I chopped a couple of Granny Smith apples and some walnuts for a salad.

Then I minced two garlic cloves, diced a small yellow onion, added the leaves from two sprigs of parsley that I'd cut up with scissors, and sautéed the mixture in a splash of olive oil. When it cooled I mixed it into ground beef and formed hamburgers. As soon as the popovers popped I'd take them out and turn the oven to broil.

The telephone rang as I was about to add dressing to the salad.

Gramma Rosa gestured that I was to answer it.

"Mikki! Why didn't you call me back?" It was Richard.

"I didn't know you'd called." I held the phone with one hand and turned the oven light on with the other so I could peek at the popovers. Almost done.

"I left you a message hours ago."

"Sorry. I haven't checked our machine." Duh. My mind had been on the funeral, the never-to-be-mentioned-again-in-my-lifetime skirt episode, my family history, and a few other issues. Not on the usual spam callers who left messages.

"How was the funeral?"

No way was I telling Richard what happened at that funeral. If I was lucky, no one even vaguely connected to anyone I'd ever met was in St. Joseph's this afternoon, and everyone who *was* there had already suffered memory loss. Plus, right now I had no privacy to talk. Gramma Rosa was in the living room, right next to the kitchen.

"The funeral was all right." I lowered my voice. "There was an open casket."

"Was that gross?"

"Sort of. Mr. B had makeup on." I wasn't going to let on how much Mr. B had not looked like himself. It didn't seem right to be talking about him that way. "What's the history assignment for tomorrow?"

"Read the next chapter. We're into the Renaissance now. Mr. Morelli was all excited about the influence of Italy on the rest of Europe."

"They developed great food in Italy," I agreed. History of food. Now *that* would be a course I could really get into.

"He was talking more about art and religion and warfare," Richard said. "Read the chapter. You'll see."

Warfare. Just the subject I needed to end my day.

"Who's on the phone?" Mom whispered as she came in. She sniffed the air and gave me a thumbs up and rubbed her stomach.

"Richard," I whispered back, before resuming my normal voice. "My mom's here. I have to finish getting dinner. Thanks for the assignment. See you tomorrow."

I put down the phone. "Dinner in about seven minutes. Onion popovers, hamburgers, apple salad."

"Mmmm. Sounds great. I love your popovers," she said. "I'll set the table."

I took the popovers out of the oven, covered them with a dishtowel to keep them warm, and turned on the broiler.

"Richard said he'd left a message," I said. "Did you check the answering machine?"

"No. I should do that," said Mom. She glanced at what I was doing. "Is there time before dinner?"

"No problem. You can delete Richard's message," I said.

"There's one more message," Mom called from the house telephone.

I heard the click of her deleting Richard's message. Then I heard another voice. One I hadn't heard in weeks. Dad's.

Chapter 20

I put the hamburgers under the broiler. Mom likes hers rare; Gramma Rosa and I like ours medium rare. I'd made Mom's a little thicker than the others.

A minute later I glanced down the hall. Mom's bedroom door was closed.

With just three of us women living here, and Gramma Rosa sometimes needing help, Mom almost never closed her door.

I flipped the burgers.

She must be calling Dad back. It must be important, or she would have waited until after dinner. It must be private, or she would have left her door open.

"Mom," I called down the hall. "Your hamburger will be overdone in another minute."

That usually got her to the kitchen. She hated burgers that weren't red in the middle. I took hers off the broiler and went to help Gramma get to the kitchen. After those three cups of tea her legs were a bit wobbly.

What were Mom and Dad talking about?

"Dinner smells delicious, Mikki," said Gramma Rosa, as I put her burger on her plate. I peeked down the hallway. Mom's door was still closed. "Your mother will be here soon enough."

I served Gramma Rosa and myself salad and one popover each,

plus our burgers. The popovers had popped just right: golden and crisp on the outside, soft and hollow inside. I broke a piece off mine and buttered it. I kept my eye on Mom's door.

Gramma Rosa looked at me quizzically. "Mikki, everyone has secrets. Your mom, too."

I didn't say anything. That certainly wasn't news after what I'd learned this afternoon.

"Even you, my favorite granddaughter. I think there are a few things you're not telling your mom and gramma." She looked right at me, as though she knew all my secrets.

What did she know? Or was she guessing?

"There are all kinds of secrets," she continued. "There are secrets everyone in the family knows, but no one talks about."

"Like why Dad left Mom and me?" I asked. "And about Grampa Sal's work?"

"No matter what you hear from anyone, your grandfather took good care of his family, and he loved your mother very much. Nothing was more important to him than family. He and your mother argued, and she went off to college out there in Washington State and didn't come home again until after he'd left this world. She never made her peace with him."

"I'm sorry I never got to meet him," I said. I meant it.

"It's a sadness." Gramma Rosa nodded. "You would have liked each other."

"What did Mom and Grampa Sal argue about?

Gramma Rosa hesitated a moment. "She didn't like his business. She was embarrassed by it, she said."

I could understand that. "Then why does she write mysteries and stories about crime all the time?"

"She told me people read mysteries to make sure evil gets punished and know there's a happy ending."

I nodded. That made sense.

"You come to me if you have any more questions. I'll tell you the truth. Or," Gramma hesitated. "I'll tell you the truth you need to know. And *that's* the truth." She leaned toward me. "You're fourteen. Old enough to know some secrets are all right to keep. Like Tony and my secret about expanding the restaurant. Like Christmas morning secrets. Other secrets, those that might hurt people, those you need to tell."

Did she know Tito and Angelo had sworn me to secrecy?

What I wanted to know right now was: what were Mom and Dad talking about? Were they getting back together? Would we be going home to Seattle?

Gramma and I had almost finished our dinners when Mom finally came into the kitchen. She didn't look happy. She sat down, hardly looking at her food.

"Your hamburger is cold," I said. "I called, but you must not have heard me."

"I was on the telephone."

As if I didn't know that. She served herself salad and took a popover and butter. She didn't seem to notice her popover wasn't warm anymore either.

"I was talking with your father."

I didn't remember her ever calling him "your father." Not a good sign.

"Oh?" I said, trying to sound as though such calls were received and made on a regular basis in our household. "How's Seattle?"

"Seattle's fine. He's fine. At least he didn't say he wasn't," Mom answered. She buttered her cold popover. "He's coming to New Jersey. He wants to see you."

"Me? Why does he want to see me?"

"Because you're his daughter. Because he hasn't seen you in almost two months."

"Doesn't he want to see you, too?"

"No. Just you."

"What if I don't want to see him unless he sees you, too?"

"That wouldn't be a good idea," Mom said. "He wants you to have dinner with him."

"Just the two of us?"

"He wants you to have dinner with him and Sung Ja and her mother."

"*What?*" He was actually bringing them here?

"Mikki, he's stopped being my husband. But he doesn't want to stop being your father." Mom's voice was eerily calm. She put a third layer of butter on her popover. She usually ate popovers plain. "Your dad thought you'd like to see Sung Ja, too."

"He told you that?"

"He's always been a good father to you, Mikki. He just wasn't a great husband."

"If he's such a good father, why hasn't he called me? Why is he living with Sung Ja and her mother?"

Mother just shook her head.

"Why does he suddenly want to see me *now*?"

"I don't know, Mikki. All I know is they're coming to New Jersey and they want to have dinner with you."

"Well, I don't want to have dinner with *them*," I declared, getting up and starting to stack the dishes. "I hate him. I hate this whole family!"

Mom sighed. "You're going to have to deal with it, Mikki. They're moving here. Your dad has a new job. In New Jersey."

"He's moving to New Jersey? And he's bringing his girlfriend? And Sung Ja?" This was too much to take in.

"Edgewood, Mikki. He said they've decided to move right here to Edgewood, so they can be close to you."

Chapter 21

Talking to Mom got me nowhere. Neither did throwing Cat into my closet as hard as I could and slamming the door.

Friday night I was going to have dinner with Dad and the woman who was breaking up our family and the girl who used to be my best friend. Every problem you could think of ... murder, family secrets, divorce, kidnapping ... had been thrown into a blender, with me on top, and someone had pushed the "chop" button. I hardly slept that night.

Then, the next morning, when I was walking to school wishing I were anyone other than Mikki Norden, living anywhere other than Edgewood, New Jersey, a car honked right in back of me.

I jumped. High. For a split second I thought I was the first fourteen-year-old in history to have a heart attack. Then I turned around.

Angelo and Tito were merrily waving to me from the windows of Tito's Cadillac.

"What are you two doing here?"

"Following you to school," said Angelo.

"You scared me half to death." Those guys were seriously weird. "Why are you following me?"

"In case you need protection," explained Tito.

I had a sudden flashback. Mom said she'd grown up with body guards. Oh, peppercorns. I was reliving the childhood she'd moved to Seattle to escape.

"I don't need protection," I said. "I'm fine. The only trouble I've had in Edgewood so far is when you two kidnapped me."

"That was before we knew about Robert Morelli," explained Tito.

"He could be dangerous," Angelo added. "Have you considered the possibility that he's your teacher because he's trying to get close to a member of the D'Andrea family?"

"Have you considered the possibility that Mr. Morelli teaches history to all the freshmen in Edgewood?" I pointed out.

Logic didn't impress these guys.

"Never underestimate the power of the Morellis," advised Angelo.

"You lived in Seattle. You don't know from New Jersey," confirmed Tito.

That was for sure. But I was learning fast. Clearly there was no point in arguing that my history teacher was not going to attack me. "He won't make trouble for me during school," I said. "Too many people around."

"Kid has a point," Angelo agreed, looking at Tito. "I told you she was no bimbo."

"When is school out in the afternoon?" Tito inquired. "We'll wait for you."

"You don't have to do that," I assured him.

"You're Sal's granddaughter. We worry about you. We don't want you to get hurt."

"You're very kind. I appreciate that," I said. Then I had an idea. "If you really want to help me, why don't you find out who was with Mr. B Saturday morning, and how he was murdered?" I leaned over and whispered through the car window. "I suspect he was poisoned. With cyanide."

"That would be unusual," said Angelo, frowning. "It is not in the Morelli tradition to use poison."

"Nah. It's too unreliable," agreed Tito. "Guns and knives are better."

"Really?" I said. "Then this is a special case. You two have the experience to figure it out. I'm only a girl. I have to be in school." I glanced at my watch. "In fact, I'm going to be late for homeroom." I turned and ran up the hill toward the school.

I didn't need my life any more complicated by having the principal call Mom to report I'd gotten to school late.

And who knew? Maybe Tito and Angelo could find out something. If the police weren't going to investigate Mr. Baldacci's murder, then maybe D'Andrea family friends would.

I might as well take advantage of my new-found criminal associations.

Chapter 22

My first day at Edgewood High School I'd sat at an empty table in the middle of the lunch room. Two girls wearing identical designer jeans had told me I was in the wrong place. That table was reserved. By them.

It didn't take me long to figure out most of the kids in Edgewood had been sitting at the same tables, with the same friends, since before The Flood. There was no place at any of their tables for a new girl in town. Namely, me.

Since then I'd sat by myself. I'd bring my lunch from home and do homework, or read Julia Child's *The Way to Cook.* She studied cooking in Paris. (Where else would I learn that the key to poaching a perfect egg is having an oval perforated egg cup? To be honest, where else would I even learn there *was* an oval perforated egg cup?) I've pretty much memorized *The Way to Cook.*

Focusing on Julia's book keeps me from thinking about how it feels to eat lunch alone because I'm the only one without a place in the school social order.

Today I sat in my usual seat, ready to open Julia, when Richard sat down next to me. I turned Santa red. Maddy Tulane and Vanessa Ride, two of the cool girls, pointed at us and giggled and one table of boys, probably the ones Richard usually ate with, craned their heads to look.

"You just ruined your reputation in Edgewood," I pointed out.

"You don't want me to eat at your table?" Richard asked.

"You're welcome," I said. "But no one's ever sat with me before." Besides, usually boys sat with boys and girls with girls. Didn't Richard understand what the other kids would say? "People are going to talk."

"Let them." Richard ignored the giggling and pointing, unwrapped a tuna sandwich and opened a plastic container of rice and something that looked like red cabbage and scallions. "You're more interesting than they are."

I sniffed. "Kimchi," I pronounced.

"You know about kimchi?" He grinned. "I sort of thought you might."

"I come from Seattle," I reminded him. "Diverse population. Asian food stores and restaurants." Not to mention that Sung Ja, my best friend until she and her mother betrayed me, was Korean-American. I looked at his lunch and sniffed. "Yours looks good."

"My mom makes it," he said. "Want some?"

"Thanks." I reached over and pulled a piece of cabbage out of the rice with my fingers and popped it in my mouth. "Hot, but not impossibly so. A balanced amount of ginger and garlic along with the hot pepper and scallions."

"All I know is it tastes like Mom's kimchi."

"I like it," I said. "Maybe your mom could give me her recipe." I looked at the rest of his lunch. "What's weird is your eating it with a tuna fish sandwich."

"Every day, since first grade, Mom's packed rice and kimchi for my lunch," Richard said. "No one in Edgewood will sit next to me when I eat it. They say it stinks. I told her I needed more than kimchi for lunch, so now she makes me a sandwich, too. So every day I throw out the kimchi and eat the sandwich. That way I'm eating what the other kids eat." He paused. "I had a feeling you wouldn't mind it."

"Not if you don't mind watching me eat left over onion popovers and blue cheese." I opened my own lunch. After a few minutes I added, "Thanks for telling me about my family on Sunday."

"I'm glad you're still speaking to me." He took another bite of kimchi and rice. "What was the funeral really like?"

"The men who meet in the back room at Baldacci's were there. I guess they're gangsters, or friends of theirs. The police were across the street. And a crew videotaped everyone who went into the church."

"Trying to identify criminals?"

Richard almost seemed too interested. Maybe he thought my life was exciting. Well, it wasn't. It was scary. But now I'd learned a little about mobsters. "Police only filmed mob funerals in the old days. The cameras were there because Mr. B's daughter-in-law's trying to convince a producer to tape a reality show at the restaurant. She wants pictures of people connected to the restaurant."

Richard whistled and waved his hands wildly for a moment in mock excitement. "Wow! A TV show filmed in Edgewood!" A few of the kids at other tables giggled. Then he lowered his hands and shook his head. "Sounds like a pretty boring show."

"That's what Gramma Rosa says. She says they're trying to dig up stuff that happened in the past. She doesn't want the show, and Mr. B didn't want it."

"Dad heard Baldacci's was going to open again this weekend. Saturday night."

"I guess that's good news," I said. "Have you gone to the police yet about Mr. B's smelling like almonds?"

"You still think he was murdered," said Richard.

"And now I have two other people working to help us prove it," I said.

"What two other people?" Richard asked.

I was ready to tell Richard when, suddenly, I decided I shouldn't share everything. It sounded pretty weird to have Angelo and Tito investigating.

"Remember, I'm a D'Andrea. I have resources," I said, teasing him a little.

"Come on. You're not for real," said Richard. Then he hesitated. "You're not, are you? I mean, you didn't even know about your family until I told you on Sunday."

I just grinned. Let him think I was kidding. If Tito and Angelo found nothing, no harm done. At least they might stay away from me for a while. I shrugged slightly, like I remembered one of the guys doing in *The Godfather*. I should watch that movie again, now that I knew my family was like their family.

"I did some research," Richard said. "I looked up cyanide on the internet. You were right. If it's in a drink it could kill someone fast, and the victim's face would get really red. Then I tried to buy some."

"You *what*?"

"I wanted to see how hard it would be for the killer to get some," he explained. "It was research."

"Oh," I said, "That was smart." I wished I'd thought of that. Maybe when this was over he and I could write an article about research methods for catching criminals.

"Cyanide isn't the kind of poison you buy to kill mice or rats in your attic. You can only buy it if you're a chemist, or you're using it for some business reason. Some chemists make it. For sure, you can't go into a hardware or drug store and buy a bottle of cyanide."

"Hmmm," I said, finishing up my last popover. "So whoever killed Mr. B ..."

"*IF* he was killed," Richard put in.

"Whoever killed Mr. B," I continued, "Had to be at the restaurant early Saturday morning. And had to be able to get cyanide." I hesitated. "Plus, he or she had to benefit from Mr. B's death. We haven't thought of anyone who fits all those categories."

"Those crazy friends of yours, the ones who kidnapped you?"

"Angelo and Tito."

"Right. You said they thought," Richard lowered his voice and looked around the lunch room before he continued, "Mr. Morelli killed Mr. Baldacci."

"That's what they said," I agreed. "Of course, we don't know if Mr. Morelli was even at the restaurant Saturday morning. All we know is he'd eaten pizza there at some time in the past, which probably most of the people who live or work in Edgewood have done. We don't have any ideas about why he'd want to kill Mr. B. Tito and Angelo thought it might have something to do with the history between the D'Andrea and Morelli families." I shook my head. "Besides, how would a high school history teacher get cyanide?"

"Actually, Mikki," Richard's voice got so quiet I could barely hear him in the noisy cafeteria. I leaned closer. "Mr. Morelli's wife teaches chemistry at the community college. She could have made it for him."

That's when the bell rang for our next class.

Chapter 23

Our next class was history, taught by possible killer Mr. Robert (Bobby) Morelli. He turned off the lights and projected pictures of Renaissance architecture and art onto the white board at the front of the classroom.

The Romans copied Greek art and columns and temples and statues. Most of the statues were of gods and goddesses who didn't have many clothes on.

Every time a naked statue of a woman was projected on the board Henry Barkman would snicker and mutter something about "great tits." The girls giggled, the boys laughed, and Mr. Morelli tried to explain how the human figure had been the subject of great art for hundreds of years and we should be old enough to appreciate that.

Henry's friend AJ whispered he sure did appreciate it, at least the boobs on the girl statues. Then the giggling started again.

The whole scene was embarrassing.

Everyone simmered down when Mr. Morelli changed the topic to Leonardo da Vinci, who was not only a famous artist, but who also invented cool stuff like submarines and helicopters, and Michelangelo, who painted the ceiling of the Pope's chapel.

Mr. Morelli was really excited about those guys. But, after all, he was Italian. They were his people. About half way through class I remembered they were my people, too, since I was half Italian. Maybe I was even related to Leonardo or Michelangelo. You never could tell.

Great cooking was an art. I kept hoping Mr. Morelli would talk about Renaissance cooking, but the only picture he had of food was in *The Last Supper.* One of the most famous suppers in history, and nobody remembered the chef.

If we had to do a paper on the Renaissance I decided I'd write about what they ate at the last supper.

While I was thinking about food, Richard was paging through a book he held in his lap, under his desk. He read several pages, tore a page out of his notebook, wrote something on it, and then he passed me a note.

> *"Poisoning was a big deal during the Renaissance. Borgia family known for it. Schools of poisoning in Rome and Venice. Most commonly used poison was CYANIDE!!!"*

Richard raised his eyebrows toward Mr. Morelli.

I shrugged my *Godfather* shrug again. (I could really get into this *Godfather* thing.) Poisoning during the Renaissance was interesting. But even if Mr. Morelli wasn't my favorite teacher, his teaching us about a time when there were schools that taught poisoning (Mom would love that! I had to remember to tell her) didn't make him Mr. B's killer. I didn't think.

Mr. Morelli turned the lights back on and raised the blinds. Vanessa Ride, who was sitting next to the window, had been doing her nails while the Power Point presentation was on.

Mr. Morelli picked up her bottle of purple nail polish and put it on his desk. More giggles.

I looked past Vanessa, out the window. There, parked right across the street from the school, was Tito's vintage Caddy.

As I watched, Tito and Angelo got out and headed toward the teachers' parking lot.

Chapter 24

What were Angelo and Tito doing at school?

Of course. They were investigating Mr. Morelli.

"Chapter seven for tomorrow," he was saying. "Don't forget to answer the questions at the end of the chapter."

I wrote down the assignment and then turned over Richard's note about the poison schools. I added,

You have to go to the police. Today.

If you'd like me to, I'll go with you.

I handed it to Richard as he passed me after the bell rang. My next class was French. (All chefs should know French. And Italian. But our school didn't offer Italian. Maybe I'd ask for a teach-yourself-Italian course for Christmas. Or maybe Gramma Rosa knew Italian and could teach me. I should ask her.)

I couldn't stop Tito and Angelo from investigating. But the police needed the information Richard and I had. They had to have a chance to make this right. I might be a D'Andrea, but I'd been away from New Jersey most of my life. I didn't totally trust Tito and Angelo.

Going to the police was the right thing to do.

Chapter 25

I don't remember what irregular verbs we were supposed to be working on in French. In Seattle I'd had French Conversation, which meant we'd talked in French, but hadn't worried much about grammar. Here at Edgewood I didn't trust that Madame Smith could order dinner in a French restaurant, but she definitely could give vocabulary and grammar quizzes.

When I opened my locker after her class a piece of green paper fluttered to the floor.

Soccer practice until 5.

Meet me after that at our usual place. R.

Richard must have stuck the note through the ventilation holes in the locker. What was the mysterious "usual place?"

It took me about two seconds to figure out he meant the library.

Very cool. Richard and I had a "usual place." Even if Tito and Angelo were watching me, who would question a student going to the library? This week it was practically my second home.

I checked the outside of the school. No Angelo or Tito. Maybe they'd stopped being my bodyguards.

Not that I needed them. But they'd said they'd see me after school. Where were they?

I started walking home.

Then I remembered Tiffany's warning. "Stay away from Baldacci's, or you'll be sorry!" I changed direction and started down the hill, toward the restaurant.

If Baldacci's was going to open again Saturday night, would anyone be there? Had Luc Baldacci hired a new manager? Had he talked with Gramma Rosa? I had to know.

I headed toward Main Street with a purpose.

Chapter 26

A dark car pulled up next to me.

I kept walking, but looked sideways out of the corners of my eyes. Either a child molester was on the loose or … just as I expected.

I didn't have to worry about where Angelo and Tito were. They'd reappeared, half a block from Baldacci's.

"So? Where're you goin'?" Angelo called out. "We looked at the school, and you wasn't there. You don't live down here."

"You don't have to drive alongside me every day," I pointed out, as the black Caddy inched along the usually quiet street next to me. Several cars honked impatiently before they drove around it. "I'm not in any danger. And school's been out half an hour. You're late."

How many people were adding "black Caddy was following Mikki Norden" to the list of strange things Edgewood thought they knew about me and my family? Embarrassed? Not me. I loved having everyone in town know men in black suits escorted me to and from school.

"We were down at Baldacci's," said Tito. "Getting some personal stuff we'd left in the back room."

"That Tiffany chick is there. And that Mrs. Baldacci. The wife of Tony's son. The one with the name like a deer," confirmed Angelo.

"Bambi," Tito added.

"Right. Whatever. They wouldn't let us into the back room. Said it was being painted."

"Painted?" I wasn't walking anymore. I was standing by their open window.

"That Tiffany mentioned that should we see you we should suggest you stop at the restaurant. She wants to see you about very important business. Right, Angelo?"

"Absolutely. She said that. But now we can drive you home, okay?" said Angelo. "So we can ensure your safety."

Tiffany wanted me to come to Baldacci's? The same Tiffany who'd threatened me at Edna's Diner and told me to stay *away* from the place? That didn't make sense.

But, then, why should this day be any different from the rest of my week?

"You can drive me home," I agreed. I really didn't have time to go to Baldacci's before I went to the library, and I should check in at home.

"So they're painting the restaurant." I climbed into the back seat and then almost climbed out again. It stank of cigarette smoke. These guys were medical miracles. They should have died of lung cancer years ago.

"They're cleaning the place up, they said," Angelo explained.

"But regarding the murder situation?" said Tito. "You can relax any remaining concerns. Depend on us. We have it totally under control. Taken care of, you might say."

"You will not require bodyguards much longer," assured Angelo.

Taken care of? I suddenly had a very bad feeling deep in my stomach that had nothing to do with the dinner hour approaching, or even with Mr. B's probable murder. "I saw you guys outside my school today," I said.

"I told you, this kid has a lot on her brain," Tito said to Angelo.

"Didn't I tell you? From inside the school, she saw that."

Angelo nodded. "We was takin' care of business. Checkin' things out."

I didn't point out to these two geniuses that if I'd seen them, half the kids and teachers at school could also have seen them. Although no one else would have known enough about them to be concerned. "What kind of business?"

"Bobby Morelli? The teacher at your school?"

"My history teacher," I confirmed. That queasy feeling in my stomach was getting worse. Of course, the stink of smoke wasn't helping. "What about him?"

"We were lookin' to see what car he drives," said Tito.

"Because?" I encouraged. We were almost at my house. Home of the dangerous D'Andrea family. Was this how Alice in Wonderland felt, trying to stay afloat in a pool of her own tears? But, unlike Alice, I wasn't getting anywhere. I had to find out what these guys were up to. Now.

"We don't want to hurt no one but him." Angelo looked at me as though I was pretty dumb to have thought anything else. "We wouldn't do that."

"But there's no reason for you to hurt Mr. Morelli!" I said. "We don't know for sure he was involved." Richard had said Mr. Morelli's wife was a chemistry teacher. Still ... even if he could have gotten cyanide ... we had no proof he was at the restaurant Saturday morning. And we hadn't found a reason he'd want to kill Mr. B. This remained an ongoing investigation.

New Jersey was still in the United States last time I'd checked. The man was innocent until proven guilty.

"Mikki, you're still learning to be a D'Andrea. This is a *Morelli* we're talking about." Tito spoke very slowly, as though teaching me to tie my shoes. "It might not be him that did Tony in, but, if it was any Morelli, then we take care of this teacher guy, and the message is delivered."

I got it then. Fast. And it might be too late to stop it. "So what did you do to Mr. Morelli?"

"We've done nothin' personally to the man himself. Not yet. Right, Angelo?"

"They're not too bright up at that school of yours, you know," said Angelo. "They write the teachers' names right on the parking spaces."

"We thought we'd have to watch for when he came out of the school and see what vehicle he got into, but we didn't even have to do that, did we?" Tito said.

"Not even that," agreed Angelo.

"So *what did you do*?" I said. Maybe it was already too late. Maybe Mr. Morelli, who spent his days teaching bored ninth graders European history, was lying dead somewhere, all because his last name was Morelli and my grandfather's last name was D'Andrea. "*What did you do?*"

"Relax, Miss Mikki. Everyone'll get home just fine today. Like you're home now." He'd pulled the Caddy over in front of my house. "You just go inside and get a good night's sleep. Have sweet dreams, like a good girl."

"We'll take care of everything!" Tito grinned. Then he actually got out of the car and opened my door for me.

Clearly I wasn't going to learn anything more from either of them now.

But it sure sounded as though they had something planned for tomorrow. Something I wasn't going to like.

Being a D'Andrea was getting more complicated every day. I definitely had to get to the library so Richard and I could talk to Chief Hunter.

Chapter 27

"Mikki? Is that you?"

Gramma Rosa was already on her second or third class of Chianti. The bottle was on the table right next to her chair, her current wine glass was almost empty, her knitting needles were silent, and an old NASCAR race was on the TV.

"Yup. It's me, Gramma." I hung up my jacket and put down my book bag. I could hear Mom's keyboard in the distance. No writers' block this afternoon. She'd be in a good mood.

"I'm glad you're home, dear. I'm getting hungry. Could you get me some crackers and cheese?"

"Sure." Managing to sample a few crackers with cheese myself, I arranged wheat crackers on a small board with pieces of cheddar and brie. (I like to serve hard and soft cheeses together, to vary textures as well as flavors.) I put the board on the table next to Gramma Rosa. Her wine glass was now full.

Gramma's hips and knees might give her problems, but her arthritis didn't prevent her from pouring.

"Thank you, dear! What are you planning for dinner?"

Dinner! I hadn't even thought about dinner. Understand: this was not normal for me. I usually plan dinner a day or two in advance. Cooking was the highlight of my day; the only time I was in control of my world. Oregano and braised meats didn't talk back to me. And if the taste wasn't just right, I could try again. No failing grades went on my record even if I burned the bacon.

Have I mentioned I love cooking?

But today I had no idea what I was going to make for dinner. And I had to get to the library.

I found mint sauce in the refrigerator. That was a start. Put potatoes in the oven (on low) to bake. Frozen peas. Simple. Not gourmet, but OK. Mint went well with peas, too.

"Gramma, I have to go to the supermarket to get lamb chops," I invented as I talked. "I forgot to buy them earlier. We're having broiled lamb chops with mint sauce, just the way you like them. I'll be back soon."

Before she could say anything I'd pulled on my jacket. I ran half the way to the library, glancing around once in a while to make sure Tito and Angelo weren't still checking on me. I didn't mind them knowing I went to the library, but they wouldn't approve of my visiting the police station.

The librarians must have spent the day decorating for Halloween. An actual skeleton was now seated, reading a book, in the reading room. Was that the right message to send about the future of reading? (Whose bones were they? Wouldn't you think they'd identify the poor fellow?) A note in his hand said he was on loan from Edgewood Hospital's anatomy department. Creepy. I hoped he wasn't a relative. Or the victim of a relative.

I picked up a copy of *Cook's* magazine and tried to concentrate on cream sauce variations but I couldn't even focus on food. I kept wondering what Tito and Angelo were planning for tomorrow. Should I warn Chief Hunter about them?

Richard arrived before I'd decided. He peeked over my shoulder. "What's for dinner?"

"Broiled lamb chops with mint sauce and peas and baked potatoes with sour cream and scallions," I said, closing the magazine. "I still have to buy lamb chops. That was the excuse I gave for leaving home. How was soccer practice?"

Richard stunk. (Not at soccer. I mean, he really smelled. Clearly he'd skipped showering to get to the library by five.) I shifted so I was a little further away from him.

"The usual. Coach Thomas worked us hard. We're playing Summit on Saturday." He pulled a stained gray hand towel out of his grungy backpack and wiped his face. "We're still going to see Chief Hunter, right?"

"It's our civic duty."

He didn't look totally convinced.

"If we don't, we could be arrested for withholding evidence," I added.

"Okay. Let's get it over with." He stuck the damp towel in his backpack.

I kept my eyes open as we walked the two blocks to the police department. Still no Tito and Angelo. Maybe they'd gone home for dinner.

The Edgewood police station didn't look like any I'd seen on television. The first thing you saw was a wall of steel bars with a desk behind it. Did they think someone was going to break *in*?

"May I help you?" said the woman behind the bars.

"We'd like to see Chief Hunter," I said.

"And you are?"

"Mikki Norden and Richard Park," said Richard.

"We're here about the Anthony Baldacci case," I added.

"Just a minute," she said. She reached under her desk. She must have pressed a secret buzzer because Chief Hunter came out from somewhere in back right away.

"Good afternoon, kids," he said. "What can I do for you two?"

I hate it when grownups call us kids, as though Richard and I were in kindergarten. If we call ourselves kids, that's different.

"We'd like to talk with you, please," I said. I looked at the woman behind the desk. "In private."

"No problem," said Chief Hunter. He pushed another button and a section of the wall of bars slid open. Richard and I followed him down a hallway into a small office. His desk was piled with notebooks, file folders and papers. The walls were covered by framed diplomas or certificates and pictures of Chief Hunter shaking hands with people I assumed were important. Richard and I sat in the two chairs in front of the desk. The chief sat on its edge.

"Yes?" He had that expression grown-ups get when they're trying to be patient, but would much rather be out on the golf course or having dinner with their wives.

"It's about the Anthony Baldacci case," I said.

"There is no 'Anthony Baldacci case,'" interrupted Chief Hunter. "Remember, Mikki? We talked about that Sunday morning. Mr. Baldacci died because his heart was old and tired. His doctor thinks so, his family thinks so, and I think so. His funeral is over, he's buried, and it's time for you to get on with your life. So unless you have new information …" Chief Hunter stood up.

"But we *do* have new information," said Richard, also standing. "We didn't tell you everything. We thought you'd figure it out. But you didn't. So we came to tell you now."

Chief Hunter sighed and sat back down.

So did Richard.

"Okay. Shoot." It was clear the chief didn't think we knew anything important. But at least he was going to listen.

I started. "When Richard and I got to Baldacci's Saturday morning the front door was locked, so we went in the service entrance. We heard a crash from upstairs."

"Then we found Mr. Baldacci. You saw him; his face was really red. I didn't tell you he smelled really bad of almonds," Richard said.

"Smelling of almonds is a sure sign of cyanide poisoning," I explained. "Someone who's been poisoned by cyanide also has a flushed face. Someone who's had a heart attack has a pale face."

"And you two are experts on cyanide poisoning because?" Chief Hunter's voice was almost too calm.

"My mom writes mysteries." I said. "Sometimes I read her books about forensics and poisons and stuff."

"You read books about poisons for fun," Chief Hunter said.

"We looked up heart attacks in the library," Richard said, ignoring Chief Hunter's tone. "After we left the restaurant we saw the front door was open. It was locked when we got there, so we went in to check. A cabinet in the bar had fallen over. Broken glasses were all over the floor. That must have been the crash we'd heard earlier. Someone else had to have been with Mr. B before we got there. Cyanide works fast. Whoever else was in the building was the one who killed him."

There. Now we'd told him everything.

Chief Hunter shook his head. "Okay. Maybe someone else was there. Maybe someone was delivering supplies to the restaurant. Or cleaning the place. I don't know. But I don't think it had anything to do with Baldacci's death. The man was old and he died of a heart attack. His doctor said so."

"But you don't know that for sure! No one did an autopsy!" said Richard. "What about the smell of almonds? What about his red face?"

"You kids watch too much television. Not everyone who dies is autopsied. Maybe the red face was from the CPR you were doing on him. Maybe he'd had a drink or two and eaten a few nuts. I saw a bottle of Grappa in his office. I don't know."

"You're not going to investigate?" I asked, incredulously. "You're not going to look for his killer, even with what we've told you?" Did he think that because we were still in school we didn't know anything?

Chief Hunter stood up. "He was your friend, and it's sad he died. He lived a long life. He died a natural death. Now, both of you, go home, do your homework, and get on with your lives. Leave crime fighting to the experts."

He wasn't taking us seriously. We headed for the door. Then Chief Hunter called after us, "Mikki, did you tell your mom I'd stopped in? She never called me."

"She's been busy," I called back.

He didn't need to know I hadn't mentioned him to her. Why did he want to talk to Mom anyway? I didn't need her knowing Richard and I were investigating a crime. She'd just get nervous and start wanting to know where I was every minute of the day. Especially given what I now knew her childhood had been like.

"That was a total waste of time," Richard said, kicking fallen leaves and acorns off the sidewalk as we left the station. "Chief Hunter thinks we're nuts."

"He's wrong," I said. "We'll prove him wrong."

"I don't know," said Richard. "What else can we do now?"

"Like he said, we'll do our homework. And right now I have to go buy lamb chops," I said. "But this case isn't closed."

I hadn't even been tempted to tell the chief about Tito and Angelo. He probably wouldn't have believed me anyway.

But he'd forgotten I wasn't just any girl. I was a D'Andrea. And no bimbo.

Chapter 28

Before I went to bed I vowed to Saint Lawrence I wouldn't give up. I was still on the case. Somehow I'd find out who killed Mr. B – and keep Tito and Angelo from hurting Mr. Morelli. I figured Saint Lawrence was connected. He might be able to help.

And at this point I could use some divine intervention.

But Saint Lawrence was the patron saint of chefs, not of private investigators. I'm sure he was sympathetic, being Mr. B's special friend and everything for so many years, but he didn't bring me any immediate inspirations.

I tossed and turned most of the night, watching the numbers on my clock radio change. I even got Cat out of the closet. Even she wasn't comforting tonight.

But maybe appealing to Saint Lawrence had made a difference.

Because by six in the morning I had a plan.

I made cheese omelets for everyone, gobbled mine, put the ones for Mom and Gramma Rosa on "warm" in the oven with some slices of defrosting cinnamon bread, and left a note saying I'd gone to school early to see one of my teachers.

I didn't say I was going to find Mr. Morelli to warn him that he might be in danger.

I could hear the school orchestra practicing in the auditorium, but no one else was around. The empty halls were spooky.

Mr. Morelli's room was on the second floor, in the front of the school. I sat at one of the desks there to wait for him.

And I waited.

And waited.

Where was the man? Didn't he want to get to school early to prepare for his students?

I watched the hands move slowly around the face of the wall clock. Seven o'clock. Seven ten. Seven fifteen. Seven twenty.

Students were in the hallways now. I heard locker doors slamming and people calling to each other.

Wasn't Mr. Morelli ever going to arrive?

What if Tito and Angelo had found him before he'd even gotten to school?

Maybe something bad happened to him at his home. Could Tito and Angelo have kidnapped him, the way they'd kidnapped me?

But Mr. Morelli was a big man. If Tito tried to push *him* out a window … I imagined Mr. Morelli stuck, half in and half out. Not a successful kidnapping. Probably a good reason Tito and Angelo wouldn't have tried it in the first place.

Would they have stopped him on his way to school? Run him off the road? They knew what his car looked like.

I started imagining accident scenes. If I'd had a cell phone I might have called 911 on general principles.

At 7:45 I finally heard Mr. Morelli's voice in the hall outside the classroom. He was alive. But it was too late to talk with him alone. How could I explain being here? He wasn't my homeroom teacher.

A door was near his desk.

I slipped inside the supply closet. Luckily I hadn't eaten too many of those creampuffs last Friday night. I fit. Just.

The closet was shallow and lined with shelves. Mr. Morelli's favorite history books from the past hundred years were stacked in there, along with notebooks and piles of paper. I could stand between the bookshelves and the door if I didn't breathe too deeply. And didn't sneeze. A dangling string tickled my face; probably a light cord. I didn't dare pull it. Someone might notice a light under the closed door.

The bell rang for home room.

The one day I'd been at school an hour early I was going to have to sign in at the principal's office and explain why I was late. Trying to save Mr. Morelli from hit men probably wouldn't fit into the usual categories of excused absences. Even if I was a D'Andrea.

Plus, for all this aggravation, I hadn't even managed to talk with Mr. Morelli.

And now that I'd gotten into the closet, how could I get out without being seen?

What would kids think if I stepped out of a teachers' closet? Not to think of what Mr. Morelli would think.

Maybe he wouldn't have a class first period. Maybe after homeroom all the kids in his the classroom would leave. Then what? I pictured myself stepping out of the closet and explaining I'd been under cover and was there to warn him. Tell him two members of my grandfather's gang thought he was part of the Morelli crime family, and were going to make an example of him.

It was the truth, but it sounded pretty lame, even to me.

I could hear the home room class filling the room, dropping their books on the desks, talking to each other. Mr. Morelli told everyone to "simmer down."

The day's announcements started blaring over the intercom. I couldn't understand what the student of the day was saying because the closet door muffled the sound. Besides, I was distracted.

My face itched where the dangling light cord kept hitting it, and my back was getting cramped. I was in a really weird position. So I don't know exactly what was being announced when

Baaaaaaaaaaaaam!

The whole closet – maybe the whole building – (how could I tell? I was in a closet!) shook. Books started falling off the shelves like dominoes. Falling on top of guess who.

Books are heavy. And this was not one or two books. This was shelves of books. I tried to cover my head, but the books knocked me down and against the door. The door didn't move. I was jammed, crouching, under an avalanche of history books. Being crushed to death, right there in the closet.

I thought for sure everyone would hear the noise of the books and find me. Then, in horror, I realized the noise of the falling books was covered by the sounds of explosions.

Students were screaming. Their screams mingled with other, smaller, explosions, like a series of Fourth of July fireworks.

The school fire alarm started blasting. In the distance Mr. Morelli was yelling, "Keep calm! Get in line! Don't panic!" The fire alarm kept going, and students kept shouting and screaming, and even in the closet, bruised and covered with books, I smelled smoke.

I freed one of my hands and started pounding on the closet door with my fist. "Help! I'm in the closet! Please! Help me!"

Then suddenly, although the alarm was still ringing and the explosions continued, the voices were gone. Everyone had left the room, as they should have in a fire drill. Left me to die buried in history books in a closet.

Triple peppercorns. I always knew history would do me in.

I banged on the door until my hand was bruised. The smoke in the closet was slowly getting thicker, seeping in along the sides and the bottom of the door, where I was, on the floor. I started coughing.

Not a good sign.

I'd heard fire safety lectures in school. You could die of smoke inhalation.

I tried to move, but books are heavy, and a lot of them were on top of me, holding me down. Every few minutes another one, perhaps teetering on the edge of a shelf high above me, fell to join the others. Old tests and maps and handouts that had fallen were filling the spaces between the books, like frosting between the layers of a cake.

I tried to stand.

There was no space. I couldn't move.

The smoke was getting denser.

I reached up. One of my hands was free. If I could turn the door knob, I could open the door and get out. I pushed and stretched and wriggled and finally slipped my right arm up through the books, onto the door. I reached for the door knob. I couldn't feel it. Somehow I had to get up higher.

If I had enough time.

Before I inhaled too much smoke.

I should put on a mask to protect my lungs from the smoke. What could I reach that I could use? I couldn't free my left arm. Or my feet. I tried to tear part of my tee shirt, but this wasn't the movies. This was real life. The tee shirt wouldn't tear.

Besides, I was wasting time.

I had to get out of there.

I could only think of one way.

One at a time I took the books still cascading down from the high shelves and tucked them underneath me, raising me up an inch or so each time. I had to get high enough to reach the door knob.

Right now I loved European history. They were the thickest books. They might have hurt the most when they'd fallen, but they raised me up the most when I pushed them underneath me.

Reach book, push under. Reach, push. Reach, push.

Try not to breathe in the smoke.

Finally, it seemed forever, but I was able to reach the door knob.

Relief flowed through me. If I could open the door I could get out.

Even if the books followed me out. Even if there were fire on the other side of the door.

I could get out.

I reminded myself of what you should do in a fire. Stay low. Feel the door to see if it's hot before you open it.

This door wasn't hot. I turned the knob. Carefully.

And, in horror, realized the door was locked.

Triple peppercorns. I was locked in a closet in a school that was on fire.

Chapter 29

I tried turning the knob again, and again, to be sure.

The closet door was definitely locked.

The school fire alarms weren't ringing as often. Maybe everyone had already escaped. Everyone but me. Fire engine sirens were sounding in the distance.

Would someone find me?

Who would look for a student they didn't know was in school today?

I tried the doorknob one more time, hoping I'd been wrong the first time. No. It really was locked. It must have locked automatically when I closed it.

If I ever got out of this place alive I had a safety recommendation for whoever built closets in schools.

My hand closed around a thin atlas with a laminated cover. One rainy day I'd read Mom's *Tips for Beginning Private Investigators*. It included advice on how to break and enter. Right now I was more interested in exiting. But this wasn't the moment to quibble. I had to get that door open.

The book had suggested using a credit card. I didn't exactly have an American Express Gold card with me. But I was desperate. I carefully slipped the thin cover of *Atlas of Civil War Battles* between the wood frame of the doorway and the door itself and moved it slowly up and then back and forth until, finally, thank Saint Lawrence, it clicked the latch.

With the weight of the books and me leaning on it, the closet door popped open.

The books and I tumbled into the smoke-filled classroom. Clouds of smoke and soot and sparks and occasional flames were blowing past the room's windows, but no flames were inside the room.

I pushed the books off, managed to stand, and stumbled through the smoke into the second floor hallway toward the closest staircase, trying to keep my head low.

Smoke filled the stairwell. I held the banister tightly, feeling for each stair with my foot. I was coughing badly. When I finally reached the first floor I put my hand on the wall of lockers I knew must be there, so I wouldn't get confused, and tried not to breathe. The smoke was as dense as fog.

I followed the line of lockers to the front door.

I walked down the front steps, bent over and took deep gulps of fresh air.

An EMT woman ran up and put her arm around me. "Are you all right? We thought everyone was out of the school!"

I nodded, still taking deep breaths. "OK. I'm OK."

"Is anyone else in there?" A fireman this time.

"I didn't see anyone," I said.

"Let me get you some oxygen," said the EMT woman.

I shook my head. "No; really. I'm OK." I was. A little light-headed, but OK. Just really, really, glad to be out of that school. And I didn't want to explain that I'd been locked in a closet. "What happened?"

"Are you sure you wouldn't like some oxygen? A car in the teachers' parking lot exploded," said the EMT. "The fire set off other cars. Now the roof of the school is on fire. Everyone needs to get away from the building. Now."

"I'm going. No oxygen," I managed to say and started to walk dizzily toward the street. A crowd of students was further down the block. I turned and looked back. Smoke framed the side and back of the school. Streaks of flames towered above the roof. Sparks flew through the air and drifted down, covering everything.

A small leaf fire broke out near the front steps I'd just left. A policeman covered it with his jacket and stomped it out.

"Hey, kid!" a fireman yelled at me. "Move further down the street! School's closed for the day!"

I kept walking.

Fire trucks from nearby towns were beginning to arrive. A WNBC helicopter hovered overhead.

I had a horrible feeling I knew whose car was the first to explode.

This whole mess was my fault.

I'd told Angelo and Tito I thought Mr. B'd been murdered. How was I to know they'd blow up the school parking lot – and maybe the school itself?

Had anyone been hurt?

Would the police be able to figure out what happened? Would they be able to trace that first explosion back to Angelo and Tito?

I blinked away tears. Maybe it was the heavy smoke in the air. Maybe there was just too much to think about. By now news of the explosions and fire was probably on the radio and television. I had to go home to show Mom and Gramma Rosa I was still alive.

And then? I wasn't sure. But I had a couple of ideas.

Chapter 30

Two news helicopters were circling downtown Edgewood like vultures looking for road kill. The sound of their engines drowned out sirens from fire engines trying to get close to the school. Local cops were re-routing traffic. Students needing transportation home were directed to the strip mall, where school buses would be waiting.

Luckily, I was a walker. A very angry walker looking for two guys who'd told me they were going to watch out for me. The same ones I needed to protect the world *from.* Had I been protected while I was locked in a closet in a burning building?

Not so much.

I rounded the corner and stopped. Tito's car was parked right in front of our house. I approached it cautiously. It was empty.

Mom and Gramma Rosa had to have heard the sirens and helicopters. Were Angelo and Tito dumb enough to tell them who was responsible?

Only one way to find out.

"Good. You're home, dear," said Gramma Rosa. She was sitting in her usual chair, the one slipcovered in a pattern of red roses. Its seat was higher than any other chair in the room, so she could sit down and stand up easily. It also meant everyone else sitting in the room had to look up to her. She was working on the Christmas afghan she'd started knitting last week. Rows of red trees on dark green were now being followed by green trees on red. It didn't look bad, just pre-seasonal. "Angelo and Tito were telling me there's been a little problem over at your school. Some juvenile delinquent left a cherry bomb under one of the teachers' cars and created quite a mess."

"Yeah," I agreed, looking at Angelo in disbelief. They already had a story in place. "They've sent everyone home for the day."

"Sounds intelligent," Gramma Rosa said, needles clicking. "Mikki, your mother wants to talk to you. In her room. Now."

Dismissed again.

What could Tito and Angelo want to talk to Gramma Rosa about now?

I assumed my usual listening position around the corner in the hall. Living here was definitely improving my eavesdropping skills.

"As we was saying, Mrs. D'Andrea. Sal, he was very good to us all those years we worked for him. Before he … went away … he fixed it so we'd still be paid regular, to make sure we'd be available should there be work needed doing while he was otherwise engaged."

"Really?" said Gramma Rosa. "How kind of Sal."

"It was. Absolutely for certain," agreed Angelo. "And those payments was very much appreciated. They came in regular. Once a month, like clockwork. In unmarked bills."

"In the mail," added Tito. "Postmarked New York, New Jersey, even Pennsylvania. Every month a different place."

"And cash, you say?" said Gramma Rosa. "Interesting. Considering Sal, of course, was incarcerated and had no access to money."

"Which we, of course, were quite aware of," said Angelo. "Which is the reason we assumed someone else …"

"Someone he trusted," put in Tito.

"Certainly," Angelo continued, "someone in the family was sending the money on his behalf."

Gramma Rosa didn't speak for a moment. "You've thought this out carefully."

"We had time. We received the dough regular for over fifteen years," said Tito.

"And ...?" said Gramma Rosa.

"After Sal, may his soul rest in peace, was shanked in the prison yard two years ago, the money didn't come so often," Tito said.

"But that would make sense, wouldn't it? Sal, being dead, would no longer require your services," Gramma pointed out.

"But the money didn't stop coming immediately, you see," Tito explained. "It came one month, and then not for a couple of months, and then maybe half another month."

"So we figured, whoever was sending the dough was getting accounts in order. Sort of a pension system reorganization, see? Then the money would go on."

"And?" said Gramma Rosa.

"It didn't," said Tito. "There've been no envelopes in six, seven months now."

"And you're telling me this, why?" Gramma Rosa asked.

"'Cause you're the closest thing to Sal that's left, and we figured you'd want to make it right," said Tito. "You know how much we did for Sal, and how he'd want to keep takin' care of us."

"I don't think you boys understand," said Gramma Rosa. "Sal never involved me in his business."

"So who had the funds?" said Angelo. "Because whoever was sending the cash had access. Maybe they even have bucks Sal would want to go to you and his daughter and granddaughter."

Tito's voice was a little louder, "If you were to tell us who that person was, we could maybe talk to them, and get the money back for you. Maybe take a little slice of it as a sort of recovery fee. To thank us for helping restore the funds to their rightful owner, as it were, you understand."

"I understand very well, Tito. But I don't know such a person. Tell me. You're intelligent men. Where did you think the money was coming from all those years? You must have had an idea."

"We figured it was Tony sending it. Sal trusted him, and he wasn't in the business, so the cops wouldn't be looking at him."

"Did you ask Tony?"

"He said he had nothin' to do with it. But he was putting a lot of money into that restaurant of his. That money was coming from somewhere."

"I'm surprised at both of you. Tony was your friend. He wouldn't have lied to you. The money for his restaurant was coming from me, not from secret money of Sal's. Neither of you boys should have been depending so much on money that came from a mysterious source."

"No, Mrs. D'Andrea." That was Tito's voice. "But it's tough. The world isn't like the old days. Some of the jobs we used to do, they're obsolete now. It's harder to find people who can use specialized skills like ours."

That, I understood. I'd seen enough movies to already figure out Tito and Angelo hadn't been the brains of Grampa Sal's organization. They'd been the muscle. Hit men can't exactly advertise on Craig's List.

I heard the wheels on Gramma's walker turn. She was getting up. "Now, I'm an old lady and I need to rest. Thank you for stopping by."

I moved down the hall toward Mom's room, where I should have been this whole time.

"Mikki!" Mom turned to me from her computer. "I heard the sirens. On TV they said there'd been an explosion at the school. Are you all right?" She looked at me closely. "You're covered with soot!"

I wiped my face with my hand. It came away black. I was glad she couldn't see the bruises I was pretty sure the cascading books had left under my clothes. A couple of days from now I was going to be very colorful. Not even counting the rope burns from the kidnapping or my elbow that was still sort of egg yolk yellow from last week's run-in with the reception desk at Baldacci's.

Living in New Jersey was tough on the body.

Luckily, this was October. Jeans and sweats covered most of me.

"I'm fine, Mom. One of the teachers' cars caught fire in the parking lot. That set off other cars. Ashes were everywhere. School's closed for the day."

Mom nodded. "So you have a day off. Perfect. Because after you clean yourself up we should go clothes shopping." I expected her to be worried. To ask for more details. To care that her daughter had almost been blown up.

"What?"

Mom never suggested we go clothes shopping. Maybe the funeral skirt fiasco had gotten to her even more than it had to me. "I'm okay, Mom. No clothes emergencies."

"What are you going to wear Friday night?"

Peppercorns. I'd been trying not to think about the Friday night dinner with Dad and the home wrecker and my former best friend.

"I told you. I don't want to go."

"You don't have a choice. Your dad has a right to see you."

"Don't I have the right to stay home?"

"No." Mom sighed. "I'm sorry, Mikki, but you don't. You have to see him. He's your father."

"A good father doesn't walk away from his daughter."

"The past weeks have been confusing for all of us. Now he wants to make it up to you."

"By forcing me to eat with him and his new family?

"Sung Ja was your friend for years. And you liked her mother, too."

"That was before. When she was just Sung Ja's mom."

"I know it's hard, Mikki. But you have to go Friday night."

I was clearly not winning this argument. "OK. So I'll see him. Them. I have clothes. I always wore jeans and tee shirts when we went out to dinner with Dad in Seattle."

"I think it would be better if you wore something a bit dressier here. Maybe a skirt and sweater."

I groaned. "Do I have to?"

Mom looked determined. "We don't want your father or … that woman … to think we're slobs, do we?"

That was it. I'd thought it was pretty dumb to dress up for your own father. It was his girlfriend I was supposed to dress up for. I'd met Sung Ja's mom lots of times. I'd eaten her cookies and kimchi. I'd had sleepovers at her house. I honestly hadn't paid much attention to her. I hadn't known she was planning to break up my family. But I was pretty sure she'd dressed up more than Mom or me.

"I'm not exactly the high fashion type."

"I'm not suggesting high fashion. I'm suggesting something other than sneakers and jeans. Girls today do sometimes wear clothes other than sneakers and jeans, don't they?"

I couldn't believe Mom was serious about this. But if you'd seen the expression on her face …

I had a lot to do. Like, finding out what Tiffany needed to talk to me about. Watching to see where Tito and Angelo went after they left our house. They probably knew Mr. Morelli was still alive and were planning another assault on the Morelli family because they weren't D'Andreas. I had French vocabulary words to memorize. I'd planned to perfect my crème brulee.

What did I do? Went shopping with Mom.

Serious shopping. We tramped through at least five different Junior departments at some gigantic mall.

Mom was focused on finding me something to wear that was "decent and classic." I was focused on not barfing. To show you how bad it was: she wouldn't even let me *look* at the kitchenware in Williams-Sonoma. That's cruel and unusual punishment. She said it was only fair: she wasn't looking in bookstores.

Neither of us was happy.

Finally I found a leather jacket and a pair of slacks and high-heeled leather boots that fit. They were actually pretty cool, although I didn't let Mom know that. She and I were weren't exactly speaking to each other by that time. I could tell Mom was doubtful, but desperate. The sales lady said the outfit was "age appropriate." Mom went along.

I may fall on my face wearing those boots. But I do have two days to practice walking before I have to wear them in public. I'll admit: they're just the sort of thing Sung Ja would love. Too bad, former best friend.

Friday night she and her mom and my dad are going to meet a never-before-seen-even-by-me version of Mikki Norden.

But I hadn't forgotten what was important. As soon as we got home I told Mom I needed some fresh air. She just nodded, wearily.

I headed for Baldacci's Restaurant.

I wanted to know why Tattooed Tiffany had changed from threatening me to wanting to see me.

Chapter 31

I knew his restaurant wouldn't be the same without Mr. B. I had no idea *how* different it would be.

Electric, flooring and painting company trucks filled the parking lot. Was Luc Baldacci modernizing the restaurant? He'd said he wouldn't be doing that. And, after all, Mr. B had only been buried two days ago.

The front door was propped open, so I walked in.

And stared.

Mr. Baldacci's wonderful, cozy, family restaurant was not being modernized.

It was being made to look old. Antiqued, I guess you'd call it.

Only the changes weren't old-and beautiful-antiqued. They were old-and-ugly. Grungy.

Two men were covering the yellow walls in the dining room with tan paint and smearing it so the walls looked decaying and dark. The walls in the lounge had already been painted a dark red and lined with old-fashioned framed black and white photographs of groups of men eating, shaking hands, and posing with their arms around each other. They probably weren't elected officials. Or, maybe they were. I wondered if my grandfather was up on that wall. Or Tito and Angelo, in their younger days. Or Mr. B.

I promised myself I'd check them out when I had time.

A couple of big guys with low-hanging pants were gluing black and white linoleum squares on top of the polished wood floor Mr. B had been so proud of. Another three men, pants pretty much in place, were hanging a wide black ceiling fan over the bar itself.

Bambi Baldacci and Tiffany had pulled several tables together and were sitting in the middle of the dining area.

"Hey, you! Out of the way!" A small man balancing a long ladder gestured for me to move.

Tiffany glanced up and waved. "Mikki! Mikki, good, you came!"

Floor plans, lists, telephone numbers, and bills covered the tables. Bambi was working at a laptop. She smiled at me, but her lined eyebrows didn't move. She winked at Tiffany and stood up. "If you girls will excuse me, I have to check kitchen supplies."

I watched her bony rear maneuver through the workers and equipment as if she owned the place.

Which I guessed she and her husband now did. Except for Gramma Rosa's share…

"What's happening?" I asked Tiffany. "Why the redecorating?"

"It's so exciting!" Tiffany said in the bubbly artificial voice she used when she greeted customers. "That's what I wanted to talk to you about! Here," she patted the chair next to her, "sit down."

I sat.

"I have the most wonderful news! It's been a secret until now. You're one of the very first to know! Mrs. Baldacci — Bambi – knows someone who's a really truly television producer, and he's thinking of developing a pilot for a show to be set right here, in Edgewood – at this restaurant! Isn't that amazing?"

Of course, I'd heard that before. I looked around. "Why all the remodeling?"

"The producer wants this place to be authentic, you know? So

Bambi's tweaking the décor so it looks more like a real New Jersey Italian restaurant."

"From the 1950's?" I asked. "It's beginning to look like a restaurant in *The Godfather* or *The Sopranos.*"

"Exactly," said Tiffany.

"But this *was* an authentic New Jersey Italian restaurant," I said. "Now it just looks old."

"Now it's the way people *think* a vintage New Jersey Italian restaurant looks," she explained. "Most people watching TV have never been to an historic restaurant like this one. Bambi's going to show them what it should look like!"

"Who's going to be in this historic television show?" I asked, already guessing her answer.

"Well," she said, sitting a little straighter. I couldn't miss her chest tattoo. "Of course, the restaurant will need a hostess, and Bambi says I fit that part perfectly." She giggled a little and patted her blonde hair. It didn't move. Then she lowered her voice and her tone got very, very serious. "Can you imagine? Getting your big break in a nothing town like Edgewood, New Jersey. Why else would I have wasted so much time here?"

She glanced around the room. "The reason I told those old guys who're always hanging around that I wanted to talk to you ."

"Tito and Angelo," I put in.

"Whoever. They were here yesterday afternoon, and mentioned they were looking out for you." Tiffany rolled her eyes. "I mean, how weird is that? But Bambi heard them, and she had the great idea that you and I should get together for a little talk. Girlfriend to girlfriend, you know."

"Really?" Girlfriend to girlfriend? Had Tiffany been sampling the stuff at the bar? Since when had she and I been more than nodding acquaintances? Very short nods, to be totally accurate.

"Bambi has this idea, you see. The producer wants his show to appeal to all ages. He thinks there should be a couple of teenagers in the cast. You, being in the D'Andrea family, and of the right age, would be perfect as the hot teenaged girl."

Me? 'Hot teenaged girl?' Did she think I was going to fall for the 'we're going to make you a star' routine? I was Mikki Norden. Not Mickey Mouse.

I waited for the hook.

"You'd come in, order pizza, and maybe ask your close friend the hostess – that would be me! – for advice about your boyfriend. Stuff like that. And maybe your boyfriend could be older, and really macho, and a member of the mob and all." She paused. "Wouldn't that be absolutely fantastic? What would your friends say if they saw you on TV?"

Was she for real? "Acting isn't exactly my thing," I said.

"You'd be a natural! I'd help you. Just be yourself!" She looked me over from head to toe. "There'd be people to do your hair, and your makeup. They'd give you clothes to wear, too."

My new BFF didn't know me very well. The more she talked the more nightmarish it sounded. But I hadn't heard the hook yet. I decided to try out my nonexistent theatrical skills.

"I'd be embarrassed to be on camera," I said, as coyly as I could manage. "All those people looking at me."

"I'd be right there beside you!" she assured me. "And your part wouldn't be all that big. At least not at first. Until you were more relaxed."

"Well, maybe," I hated myself for allowing her to think for even a moment that I might consider this total idiocy. Now, if the part had been as a sous-chef …

"There's just one teensy weensy little bitty problem that might get in the way of all these wonderful plans," Tiffany confided.

Here it came. "Oh?" I asked.

"Your dear grandmother. Did you know she owns part of the restaurant now? She and Mr. Baldacci were such good friends that she gave him a few dollars so he could make some minor changes here. Unfortunately, they're not the same changes the television producer wants."

"Really?" I said, pretending this was all new information.

"Of course, Bambi and Luc Baldacci would like to give your grandmother back her money. Then all the contracts your grandmother and the late Mr. Baldacci signed can be ended. Your grandmother doesn't seem to understand how easy this can be."

"She doesn't?" I asked, trying to look dumb. "You mean she just has to take her money back?"

"And sign a few papers, of course. Legal stuff. I'm sure you and I couldn't understand it," she assured me. "If she doesn't do that, then Bambi and Luc will have an obligation to all those people who were going to add on to the restaurant. And, most important, without your grandmother's permission they won't be able to use the restaurant for the television show."

"So you want me to talk her into signing the papers."

"Tell her they're willing to buy her out, of course. And maybe even find a tiny role for her in the television program, too! But it would probably be best for both of you if she just took her money back and stepped away."

"Why would it be best for her?" I asked, wondering how high Gramma Rosa's blood pressure would go if she were offered a role in this proposed reality show. (Which sounded pretty scripted, the way Tiffany was describing it. But, then, what did I know about reality shows that weren't about cooking?)

"Just give her the message," said Tiffany. Her tone had changed. She wasn't giggling. Or asking. She was definitely delivering a threat.

I didn't get a chance to answer. Because at that moment my other dear friends Tito and Angelo walked in.

"Hey! I hear youse need some Italian actors for a television program. We could be very authentic, guaranteed. And, guaranteed, no one would bother anyone working at this location," said Tito. "We're experts at that kind of work, right Angelo?"

"That's it," said Angelo, hitching his pants up a little under his bouncing stomach. "Very experienced. And it happens we're in need of jobs just now, so we're available."

"How you doin', Mikki?" Tito looked at Tiffany and then at me. "Maybe we could give you a lift home or something?"

I turned to Tiffany. "If the Baldaccis want to talk to my grandmother they should contact her lawyer."

Tiffany started to sputter. I didn't wait to hear what she was trying to say. I turned to Tito. "Thanks for the offer of the ride. I'm finished here."

Chapter 32

"So, what did that Tiffany want with you?"

For once, I felt comfortable answering Angelo. "She wants me to convince Gramma Rosa to sign off on her share of Baldacci's. They're trying to convince a friend to produce a reality television program there."

"Rosa's hanging them up?"

I nodded. "Mr. B didn't want the TV show and neither does Gramma Rosa. After the funeral she told Mr. B's son to call her lawyer." I hesitated. "I think Tiffany just wants to be a star. But she was coming on pretty strong. She was almost threatening Gramma Rosa."

"You want we should take her out?" Tito asked, casually.

"You mean, kill Tiffany?" I was catching on to this family stuff. "No! But now I'm worried about Gramma."

"We'll protect her," Angelo promised. "Like we protect you. You and Rosa and your mom are Sal's family. We won't let nothin' bad happen to any of you."

Tito pulled his car up in front of my house.

"Will you leave Mr. Morelli alone now?" I asked.

"We talked it over. We decided you was right. We need more proof." Angelo raised his hands in front of his chest, palms out.

"For right now, we don't touch Morelli," Tito promised.

"Or his car? Or his house?" I asked. I was getting smarter at asking these guys specific questions.

"We won't do nothin' to him. 'Course, if your teacher's smart, he'll know why the fire started with his car," Angelo added.

"If he doesn't have sense, one of his relatives will most likely clue him in," said Tito. "He's not the only Morelli in New Jersey."

"But nothing's going to happen tonight," I said. "Nothing bad. Promise me." What if Mr. Morelli was like me? A regular person born into an irregular family.

"Tonight we'll keep an eye on your house," said Angelo. "In case someone gets ideas about Rosa. Or about any of you."

"Good," I nodded. "But you guys won't do anything crazy yourselves."

"Nah," said Tito. "It's been a long day."

No kidding. The smell of gasoline smoke from the fire in the school parking lot still hung in the air as I walked from their car to my house.

Car bomb, school evacuated, my first really high heels, Baldacci's restaurant turned into a movie set, and in forty-eight hours Dad arriving with replacements for Mom and me.

A typical Wednesday in suburban New Jersey.

I was ready for what I thought was going to be a quiet evening.

But, peppercorns, was I wrong. Again.

Chapter 33

At first all was peaceful at home.

Mom was glued to her computer and Gramma Rosa was settled in her big chair knitting green trees, sipping red wine, and watching The Weather Channel.

I put a large pot of water on to boil and started grating leftover cheeses: Swiss, two kinds of cheddar, parmesan, and gruyere. Mix them together with some dry mustard, black pepper, a touch of cayenne and cooked whole wheat macaroni, put them in a casserole dish, add just enough milk and we'd be set for a mac and cheese main course.

Simple, nutritious, soothing ... and one of my favorites. Homemade macaroni and cheese is totally different from that stringy orange stuff you buy in a box. Ugh.

It's easy, too. I had the casserole in the oven in fifteen minutes. While it was baking I sliced and fried four small zucchini.

While my hands were grating and mixing and frying, my mind was on what was happening outside my kitchen. Would school be open tomorrow? How much damage had the fire done?

I peeked out a front window. Tito's car was parked down the street. He was keeping an eye on us, just as he'd promised.

Good. I wondered if the police were keeping an eye on him. After all, he and Angelo *had* tried to blow up Mr. Morelli this morning, and, although they'd failed at that, most of the teachers were probably driving rental cars tonight.

"I understand you got some new clothes today. That's a good thing," Gramma Rosa said during dinner. "And I like how you fried the zucchini, Mikki. You have a gift for cooking."

"Thanks," I said, serving myself more macaroni and cheese. Comfort food: something I could definitely use tonight. Next stop: a hot bath. My body was beginning to ache. How many bruises would show up tomorrow? Pretty soon my entire body would be purple, blue or yellow. I gave Mom a sort of sidewise smile. Those boots she'd bought me *were* pretty cool. "Mom wants me to be a fashion plate Friday night."

"About time, you know," said Gramma Rosa. "Won't hurt you to get a little dressed up. Could be fun."

"I guess." I admitted.

"If you feel good, you'll look good. Isn't that true, Cate?"

"That's what you always say, Mother," Mom answered, glumly picking at her macaroni and cheese. Either she was still having trouble killing off Frankie, or she, too, was worried about Friday night. Sometimes it was hard to tell the difference between Mom's real problems and problems in her fictional worlds.

Me, my problems were all too real. And no outfit in the world could make me enthusiastic about Friday night. Although later tonight I might try on those boots again and practice walking around a little. Maybe they'd make me feel taller. That might be fun. A new perspective on the world.

"I happened to walk by Baldacci's when I was out this afternoon," I said, changing the subject and only fudging the truth a little.

Immediately I had both Mom's and Gramma Rosa's attention.

"A lot of construction trucks were in the parking lot," I said. "I was curious so I went inside to see what was happening."

"Oh, Mikki, you shouldn't have done that," Mom groaned. "Mr. B's gone. You don't know who might be there now. Besides, you can't just walk into a construction site. It might be dangerous."

If she only knew.

"Let the girl finish," interrupted Gramma Rosa. "That restaurant is mine, too. I should know what Tony's son and that cartoon character wife of his are up to."

"She was there. Bambi Baldacci," I continued.

"That's the one," Gramma Rosa nodded. "Watch out for her. She's sneaky. She's wants to bring notoriety to this town."

"She's changing everything, Gramma Rosa," I said. "She's making the restaurant look like a scene in an old movie. The walls are painted to look old, and they're putting down ugly fake tile floors, and adding ceiling fans, and hanging old photographs on the walls."

Gramma Rosa put down her fork. "Old photographs? Of what?"

"I think they're of Mafia people from the old days, like back in the sixties and seventies. Maybe the eighties."

The lines and wrinkles in Gramma's Rosa's face became deeper and harder, as though someone had modeled her in wet clay and let the clay harden without smoothing the edges.

"Are you all right, Mother?" asked Mom.

"No, I am *not* all right," said Gramma, getting up, and turning her walker toward the living room. "I am furious. That idiot – that *Bambi* – is doing to Tony's restaurant exactly what Tony did *not* want done. I can't let this happen! Mikki, get me my telephone. I need to talk to my lawyer. And if that doesn't work, I need to make other arrangements."

Whoa! 'Other arrangements' didn't sound good.

I ran and got her the cell phone she usually left in her bedroom.

"Now, both of you, leave me alone. I need to talk. And I'm going to say some nasty words I don't want you hearing an old lady using," said Gramma Rosa. She plunked herself down in her chair in the living room. "Don't worry yourself about doing the dishes now, Mikki. They'll wait. This call will not."

Mom put her arm around my shoulders and herded me away.

"Is she going to be all right?" I asked.

"Don't worry," Mom said. "She's upset. She'll calm down. She may not even be able to reach her lawyer at this time of night."

"Maybe I shouldn't have told her," I said. "But the restaurant looked awful!"

"It isn't your fault. She would have found out. But let's make double sure she takes her blood pressure meds tonight. She's going to need them."

"Since I can't clean up the kitchen, may I call Richard? He lives near the school. I want to know how bad the fire turned out, and whether we have school tomorrow."

Mom nodded. "Go ahead. Take the house phone into your room."

Richard answered. "It's a mess! I went over there an hour ago to see. The school and parking lot are still blocked off. I think all the cars in the teachers' lot burned."

"Wow. What about the school?"

"Part of the roof's gone. It's lucky the outside of the building is brick. Some bushes and trees around the school burned, but I think the building is pretty much okay. Classrooms on the parking lot side are probably messed up, though. Especially those under where the roof burned. That's probably why they've cancelled classes for the rest of the week."

"No school at all?"

"Home room mothers are calling. We shouldn't stay on the phone long if you haven't gotten your call yet. They want to make sure everything's safe and clean before we go back. I'll bet most of the teachers will have to get new cars, too."

"Do they know how the fire started?" I asked, warily.

"I don't think so. Someone guessed one car had a leaking gas tank that caught fire. Or maybe a teacher left a burning cigarette in the parking lot. Someone else said a student put a pipe bomb under one of the cars. Dad heard the fire department called in the ATF in Newark to figure it out."

"The ATF? That's a Federal Bureau. Why the big guns?" Shoot. Maybe no one knew yet it all started with Mr. Morelli's car. I decided not to tell Richard. "Was anyone hurt?"

"A couple of firemen got minor burns. No serious injuries. You can still smell the smoke. I guess they called in the ATF because they think there might have been a bomb involved."

"Right," I said. "Of course." ATF. Alcohol, Tobacco, Firearms and Explosives. Did those guys cover racketeering too? Would the FBI have files on people like Angelo and Tito? Today most law enforcement agencies cross-checked their files, didn't they? My education-via-mysteries hadn't covered everything. Mom would probably know. But I wasn't going to ask her.

"What did you do all day?"

I briefly told him about shopping with my mom and then visiting Baldacci's. I left out the part where Angelo and Tito offered Gramma Rosa and me protection. I wasn't sure Richard would understand about them. Especially since they were the two who'd kidnapped me a couple of days ago. Not to mention what they'd done at school that morning.

I wasn't sure I understood them myself.

"Hey, Mikki. I was thinking. Maybe if we went back to the restaurant we could find a clue that would help us figure out who killed Mr. Baldacci. You said the building's open, and all those people are wandering around. Since we have no school for the rest of the week, we have time."

"Tomorrow morning. 9:00. Meet at Edna's?"

"Got it!"

I opened my door slightly. I didn't hear Gramma Rosa's voice. She must have finished yelling at her lawyer.

I headed for the kitchen to clean up. "I'll get your good night pills, Gramma," I said.

She didn't answer.

She usually complained when I mentioned getting her pills.

All at once I had the feeling something wasn't right.

I went to her chair.

Gramma Rosa was slumped over, hardly breathing. Her eyes were closed, and her skin was pale. Her cell phone lay on the floor on top of her knitting.

Strangely, she smelled of turpentine.

"Mom!" I yelled, "Mom, come quick! Something's happened to Gramma Rosa!"

Chapter 34

For the second time in a week I dialed 911.

Mom loosened Gramma Rosa's shoes and blouse and gathered up her medications, her insurance cards, and a list of her doctors. I found sweaters for Mom and me, and Mom's pocketbook and car keys.

The EMTs took four minutes to reach our house. Minutes after that Gramma Rosa was on oxygen, under blankets, and on her way to the hospital.

Mom and I followed in our car.

Dad left. Mr. B died. Now Gramma Rosa … It wasn't fair. She couldn't die. I was just getting to know her.

And it was all my fault. I shouldn't have told her what was happening at the restaurant. She was pale: maybe she'd had a heart attack. Maybe her blood pressure had gone way up because she was upset. My mind filled with horrible possibilities. I hardly noticed when we pulled into the Edgewood Hospital emergency room parking lot.

Gramma Rosa was already back in a room where I hoped doctors and nurses were working miracles. I stood close to Mom while she filled out insurance forms and made sure the doctors had Gramma's medical history.

The hospital corridor smelled. Bleach, and pee, and vomit, and sweat, and stale air, all melded together. Sort of like when you sauté vegetables and none of them taste exactly like themselves anymore. Together they taste like something totally different and, you hope, better. The hospital smell was totally not better.

Mom squeezed my hand. Normally that would be the last thing in the world I'd want. Tonight I squeezed back.

We waited outside the emergency room for what seemed forever. CNN was on the television hanging from the ceiling. I could have taken a test on the current situation in the Middle East and how the president was expected to react to it and who was speaking at the United Nations tomorrow and how that would affect the traffic situation in New York City.

Mom and I sat like those fashion dummies in the mall stores we'd walked through earlier.

We didn't talk. We just stared at that box hanging from the ceiling. I felt tears in back of my eyes. Waiting there. Just in case.

The national weather map was on for the fifth time when a woman in a pea-green coat came out from the treatment area. "Rosa D'Andrea's family?" she asked.

Mom and I stood up.

"Come with me, please," she said. We followed her through swinging doors back into the emergency room. Doctors and nurses were working at a circular desk in the center of a large room. Patients were lying on stretchers or beds separated by curtains. Some were in small cubicles along the walls.

Where was Gramma Rosa?

The woman in the green coat stopped just outside the cubicle furthest from the main desk. I peeked around her. Gramma Rosa was lying on the bed inside. She looked very small and old under a white sheet. An oxygen mask was over her nose and mouth, and a needle in her arm was attached to a tube and a bottle hanging above the bed.

She didn't look like the same woman who'd been yelling about Bambi Baldacci when we were eating dinner.

"I'm Dr. Samantha Rander. We believe Mrs. D'Andrea is going to be all right."

My mind held on to those words as though they were pieces of gold. "Going to be all right."

Dr. Rander was still talking. "Pulse weak, fast heartbeat, irritation of bronchial tubes, and possibility of complications. We'll need to keep her here at least overnight to make sure her body has been able to throw it off completely."

"I don't understand," Mom was saying. "What caused this?"

"She breathed an irritant which caused her to pass out," said the doctor.

"She was fine just minutes before!" I said.

"I can only discuss her medical condition," said Dr. Rander. She looked over Mom's shoulder down the hall. "But any time we suspect poisoning we have to report it to the police. In a few minutes a detective will be here to speak with both of you."

Chapter 35

Detective Robert Adler might have been a nice enough guy if you'd met him at a barbecue. Mom and I met him in a small cubicle in a smelly hospital where, basically, he was asking us why we'd poisoned Gramma Rosa. Not a good basis for friendship.

First he took forever to establish our names and ages and relationships.

Yes, I was Mom's daughter, and yes, she was Gramma Rosa's daughter, and yes, we all lived together.

Yes, we all got along well.

This was definitely not the time to mention Mom and I didn't always agree on curfews, or Gramma Rosa and Mom had different opinions on clothes. We were a wonderful, close, loving family. You don't have to be an expert on murder mysteries to know it's important to give the right answers when a detective's asking.

Then we got to the fun stuff.

Yes; Gramma Rosa was Salvatore D'Andrea's widow.

Long pause.

Yes; *that* Salvatore D'Andrea.

Yes; Mom was separated from her husband, who lived in Seattle.

No; she didn't know where he was at this exact moment. (Dad? Poison Gramma Rosa? Was this guy for real?)

Yes; Mom could provide Dad's telephone number.

Where had we been for the past several hours? All in the same house. When Gramma Rosa collapsed we were in different rooms. Why? (Did he think we should be joined at the hip?)

Gramma Rosa was on the telephone. Talking to whom? Mom gave him the name of Gramma's lawyer.

I was also on the phone, so I gave him Richard's name. (Richard's dad was going to love it if the police called to verify my whereabouts tonight. That would really prove my solid citizen status.)

What had we done today? We told him our schedules. He seemed very interested that I'd been at Baldacci's restaurant where they were doing renovations.

Finally I was able to ask a question. "How could Gramma Rosa be poisoned? She ate the same dinner Mom and I did. I made it, and we ate together. *We* didn't get sick."

The detective looked from one of us to the other. "The doctors don't think your grandmother was poisoned by anything she ate or drank. They think she inhaled something that irritated her lungs and affected her breathing."

"Maybe the smoke from the fires at the school today? A lot of people were coughing from that. She's old; maybe the smoke bothered her more than it bothered other people." I was trying to figure out what had happened.

Detective Adler shook his head. "Smoke inhalation wouldn't cause the reaction your grandmother had, although several people came to the emergency room today with smoke-induced asthma. No; the doctors think she inhaled something like bleach, or turpentine. It had to be held very close to her face for her to pass out so quickly."

How many days ago had Tito and Angelo held something over my face? Where were they now? They'd promised to protect Gramma Rosa. Right now I was tempted to tell the police about my mini-kidnapping. But I hadn't told Mom about that. I decided not to mention it now.

Mom frowned. "Why didn't you just ask us, Detective? There's bleach in our laundry room. I don't know if we have turpentine. We haven't painted anything since Mikki and I moved in. If there is turpentine, it would probably be in the garage. Mother – Mrs. D'Andrea – would know. But I promise you neither Mikki nor I held a cloth over my mother's face."

"Was the door of your home locked or unlocked?" asked Detective Adler.

Mom turned to me. "Mikki, did you lock it when you came in before dinner?"

"I don't remember," I admitted. Had I made that major mistake? Was it my fault Gramma Rosa was in the hospital?

"Is there anyone who'd want to harm Mrs. D'Andrea?" asked the detective.

Mom and I looked at each other. Mom knew Gramma Rosa was angry at Bambi and Luc Baldacci. I knew Tiffany and Bambi were angry at Gramma Rosa. Tiffany'd threatened her just this afternoon. But poison her? What should either of us say?

"My mother owns part of Baldacci's restaurant. Anthony Baldacci, the other owner, died a few days ago and she disagrees with his son about how it's going to be managed now," said Mom. "That's the only problem I can think of. She's an elderly woman, detective, and she's partially disabled. She doesn't even leave the house often."

Detective Adler wrote something down and then closed his notebook. "Thank you both. You've been very helpful. Dr. Rander tells me Mrs. D'Andrea will need to stay here at least overnight. I'll talk with her before she's released. She may remember what happened. I'll follow up on the information you gave me. In the meantime, this is an open investigation."

Translation: Mom and I were both still suspects.

Chapter 36

Mom and I didn't get home until after midnight. The message that school was cancelled for the rest of the week was on our answering machine. Mom agreed the dirty dishes in the kitchen could wait until morning. We were both exhausted.

When I dragged myself to the kitchen at seven the next day Mom was already up. Coffee was brewing, and she'd washed the dishes.

"I couldn't sleep," she admitted. "How're you doing, Mikki? Really. This past week has been incredible."

I poured myself some OJ. "I'm okay. Are you going back to the hospital right away?"

"As soon as I have some breakfast," Mom said. "I was about to make myself a fried egg sandwich."

"I'll make it," I said. "Thanks for cleaning up." I pulled out the eggs and put a couple of slices of bread in the toaster. "Do you mind if I don't go with you this morning? I promised to meet Richard. If Gramma Rosa comes home, I'll see her later."

"That's fine. I may have to wait around a while at the hospital. Sometimes it takes a long time to get the paperwork together before they release someone. If they don't let her come home today, you can go back with me to visit her this afternoon or tonight." Mom paused. "Why don't you take Gramma Rosa's cell phone with you today?

That way I can get in touch with you if I need to."

I almost dropped the egg shells into the frying pan. Mom was letting me take a cell phone? Even if it was Gramma's, this was a major breakthrough. Mom must be really worried.

"Thanks," I said.

I put our fried egg sandwiches on the table. "I wonder what Gramma Rosa will tell Detective Adler."

"That's what I keep thinking about," said Mom. "After all the mysteries I've plotted, here we have one in our own house, and I'm not sure I want to know the answer. How could someone come in here without either of us hearing them? And why?"

I doubt if either of us tasted our breakfast sandwiches. Mom was probably thinking of installing new locks, I was thinking of Angelo and Tito. They'd said they'd protect us. Where had they been when we'd needed them last night? Had they lied to me about protecting Gramma Rosa?

Come to think of it, where were they right now? I wanted to pop up and look out the window, but I didn't do it when Mom was there. Tito and Angelo might be Gramma's friends, but they were my secret.

"I went around the house early this morning and checked. Every window is locked. After I leave, double lock the door, won't you, Mikki?" said Mom, taking her empty plate and coffee cup over to the sink. "When you go out, be sure you lock the door behind you. And don't let anyone in while you're here alone."

"I won't, Mom. Promise."

She didn't need to tell me to check the lock on the door. I checked it three times after she left. Tito's car was in the same place it had been yesterday afternoon: across the street, down a couple of houses.

Knowing that, I felt safe enough to shower. I turned the shower pressure on "gentle" so the water wouldn't hit my bruises too hard and put Gramma Rosa's cell phone on the shelf over the sink, just in case I needed it.

After that I wandered around the house for a while. I couldn't settle down, and it still wasn't time to leave for Edna's.

The morning show on the TV was covering yesterday's fire. "Investigators suspect arson in the largest car fire in recent history yesterday in the small residential town of Edgewood, New Jersey," the announcer was saying. They showed helicopter shots of the burning parking lot. "Twenty-seven vehicles were destroyed, and damage to the Edgewood High School totaled more than $300,000. The school will be closed until the roof and several classrooms can be repaired. Anyone with information about the origin of the fire is urged to call the Edgewood Police Department at ..."

I turned the television off. I knew who'd caused the fire. They were sitting right outside my house. Or at least down the street. But Chief Hunter hadn't believed me the last time I'd told him about a possible crime. Why would he believe me now?

Life had been so simple when I'd lived in Seattle with Mom and Dad.

Dad.

Tomorrow night I had to see Dad. And Sung Ja. And her mother.

What was I supposed to do? Welcome them to the beautiful, sleepy little town of Edgewood, where nothing ever happened?

Even they would have heard about the fire.

Brrrrrring.

I jumped.

I'd put Gramma Rosa's cell phone in the pocket of my jeans, but I wasn't used to hearing it ring so close to me.

"Hello?"

"Just checking to see if you'd remembered the phone." It was Mom.

"It was in my pocket."

"Good! Gramma's much better. She can breathe without extra oxygen, and her heart rate is down. After Detective Adler talks with her they'll decide if she can come home today."

"Did she say who poisoned her?" I asked.

"She won't tell me," said Mom. "She said she'd tell the police, but she didn't want me to worry."

"She thought that would make you feel better?" I asked.

"Gramma Rosa has her own way of doing things," said Mom. "You take after her that way."

"Very funny," I said. "When will Detective Adler get to the hospital?"

"He left a message that he'd be here in half an hour."

At least when Gramma talked to the detective she could tell him who broke into our house. Mom and I would be off the suspect list.

I decided to fill my time looking at old photos. Gramma wouldn't mind; she loved showing me pictures of when Mom was young. I opened the drawer of her dressing table where I knew she kept them.

Underneath the photos was a stack of envelopes. They were empty and unstamped, but addressed. Half were addressed to Tito Piccolo; half to Angelo Serio.

Those mysterious cash-filled envelopes Angelo and Tito had talked about. Gramma Rosa must have been sending them all those years.

But there was more in the drawer.

Under the envelopes was a handgun.

I put the envelopes and the photographs back, very carefully. I didn't touch the gun.

Gramma Rosa was right. Everyone had secrets.

Chapter 37

Every time I thought I knew more about Gramma Rosa it seemed I knew less.

Dad's parents died before I was born, so she was my first grandmother experience. Maybe she'd caught me off guard because she knit, and drank tea, and used a walker, like grandmothers in books and movies. And she listened to me, and seemed to like having me around.

But she'd also been paying off friends in the mob, and she kept a gun in her dressing table drawer. This was not normal grandmother behavior.

Plus, having bodyguards who'd tried to kill my history teacher was not giving me a warm fuzzy feeling. What good had Gramma Rosa's gun been last night? Someone had broken in and poisoned her.

Why was all this happening? Why couldn't I just be a normal girl with a normal family, the way I'd been in Seattle?

Although that hadn't worked out too well either.

I was tired of all this.

Whoever was messing with my friends and family had better stop.

I didn't know what I could do about it, but I was going to do something.

And I'd be safer if I depended on myself, not on two old guys I hardly knew.

I didn't have a gun. (Believe me, I didn't *want* a gun.) But at least today I had a cell phone. I touched the phone in my pocket for good luck. Maybe I should put 911 on speed dial.

I didn't care if this was the way life was in New Jersey. This wasn't the way I wanted to live.

As usual, I got to our meeting place before Richard did. I ordered a vanilla milkshake and waited. Every few minutes I touched my pocket to make sure Gramma Rosa's cell phone was still there.

Richard slid in across from me. "Good morning!"

"You seem happy and full of energy this morning," I grumbled.

"You're not?" he said. He stared at my shake. "Milkshake for breakfast?"

"Calcium. Sugar. Food of champions." I flexed my arm in his direction. "Besides, I already had breakfast at home."

"Okay, okay." He ordered French toast.

"We've got all day," he said, pouring about a pint of maple syrup over his French toast. The boy was a sugar and carb freak. "Not even homework to worry about. I assume no exciting developments at your house? Or maybe you were kidnapped by aliens last night? Or the mob took over your basement as their new hideaway?"

I looked him straight in the eye. "Someone broke into our house and poisoned my grandmother. She's in the hospital right now being questioned by the police."

"All right, Mikki," he grinned. "I'm sorry. You have to admit an amazing number of strange things seem to happen to you and your family. What really happened last night?"

"Sorry my life weirds you out. I was at the hospital with my grandmother, like I said. She was unconscious, so the police questioned Mom and me to see if we were the ones who'd poisoned her." I watched Richard's face change as he began to realize I wasn't joking. "By the way, you were my alibi. I was talking to you on the phone when it happened. So if the police call later to ask when you talked to me, make sure you back me up."

"No kidding?"

"No kidding." I finished my milkshake with a noisy slurp. "My life. A drama a day."

"I'm sorry, Mikki. Really. How is your grandmother?"

"Better. She's supposed to come home this morning, after she talks to the police and the doctor checks her again."

"How'd someone break in?"

"I may have left the door unlocked," I admitted. "Gramma Rosa was in the living room; Mom and I were in our bedrooms. I found her after I talked with you."

"Did someone give her poison to drink?" Richard frowned, not understanding.

"The detective said she breathed the poison. Something like bleach or kerosene." I hesitated. "When I was kidnapped, Angelo and Tito put something that smelled bad over my face. Maybe something like that."

"You told me they'd drugged you," Richard remembered.

"I was unconscious for a while. So was Gramma Rosa."

I kept going back to Tito and Angelo. Where had they been when they were supposed to be watching the house?

Richard shook his head. "It sounds like the same thing. Did you tell the detective about your being kidnapped?"

"I haven't told anyone but you."

"It's time you did, Mikki. People aren't supposed to keep things like being kidnapped a secret."

Regular people didn't have lives like mine. "I'll think about it," I said. "First we're going to Baldacci's. You know they're tearing the place apart now."

"The whole place?" Richard asked.

"Maybe not the offices and kitchen," I told him. "I just saw the dining room and lounge area. They're into big-time redecorating. You won't recognize it. Mr. B wouldn't recognize it."

"We don't need to search the dining room or lounge. We found Mr. Baldacci in his office. He must have fallen from his chair, since all those papers were on the floor."

"Right," I agreed.

Only a week ago I'd gone to Baldacci's restaurant and borrowed mascarpone. I'd been much younger then.

"Cyanide works fast. Whoever poisoned Mr. Baldacci probably put it in his coffee right there in his office, maybe when he turned around to look at something, or pick up his telephone."

"Okay," I agreed. "But what evidence do you think we could find there now, five days later?"

"I don't know," said Richard. "But the police didn't even examine this place. It can't hurt to try. We'll look for anything that might be a clue about whoever killed him."

We headed out into the brisk fall morning. Most Edgewood students were probably sleeping in, enjoying their unexpected day off from school.

Richard and I were in search of evidence we hoped would lead to a killer.

Chapter 38

Baldacci's parking lot was full. The trucks that had been there yesterday were back. Richard and I went around to the service entrance, the way we had that awful morning we'd found Mr. B. The back door was unlocked, just as we'd hoped.

The painters and plumbers were changing the restaurant, not the kitchen. Maybe they wouldn't even see us.

The door to Mr. B's office was closed. Richard bent down to look under it. "No light under the door," he whispered, in case someone else was downstairs.

I knocked, to be sure. No one answered. I turned the knob. The door wasn't locked.

We went inside and closed the door.

Mr. B had been so happy in this office. Now it was almost as though he'd never been there.

Someone, probably Luc or Bambi Baldacci, had started to go through his papers. Stacks of files and notes were piled on the desk and credenza. The photos of Mr. B with famous people who'd eaten at the restaurant were gone. Maybe they'd reappeared on the walls upstairs. Recipe books and restaurant equipment catalogs were stacked in the corner.

I wondered if they were going to be thrown out. I'd love to study them.

But now wasn't the time.

Richard started opening the desk drawers. Most were empty.

"Here are his business files," said Richard. He pointed at a deep drawer full of file folders. "Files for each of his employees. Maybe he had trouble with someone who worked here."

"Most of them had been here a long time," I said. "Gramma Rosa once said working at Baldacci's was like having a job for life."

"Not everyone working here was old," Richard pointed out.

"No." I picked a leather bound calendar up off the desk. "We should check his appointment book. Maybe he expected someone to visit him late that Friday night or early Saturday morning."

"I'll take the calendar," Richard said. "You know the people who worked here. Look through the files and see if he hired anyone recently. Or maybe there'd be notes in a file. A reason someone had a problem with him."

"Got it."

I sat on the floor. Some of the file folders were so old they were faded. Only two were new. John Chou, who worked in the kitchen. He'd been recommended by a friend of Mr. B's who lived here in Edgewood and was working part-time while attending community college and studying computer science. No notes about problems. I put his file back.

The other new file was for Tiffany Schuman. Tiffany! Her file had a note clipped to it, dated seven months ago. "Do me an enormous favor and hire this dear friend of mine. She'll do a great job for you! Bambi." Of course. She was Bambi's friend. I skimmed her employment application. "Richard! I think I found something!"

"What? The guy lived a pretty boring life as far as I can tell. I can't find any appointments that look suspicious or interesting." He closed the appointment calendar and put it back on the desk.

"Tiffany, the restaurant hostess? She was hired because Bambi Baldacci recommended her."

"She's the blonde? The one with the ..." He didn't look at me. "The generous figure."

"That's the one," I said. "And that's it. She's may not be such a bimbo. Her employment application says she has a degree from New York University. She worked for a couple of drug companies when she was in college. And guess what she majored in?"

Richard shrugged. "Drama?"

"Chemistry."

Chapter 39

The office door burst open.

Bambi Baldacci stood in the doorway. "Mikki Norden! What are you doing here? What right do you have to be messing around in this office?"

I slipped Tiffany's file back into the drawer. "We have the day off from school," I said. "Because of the fire yesterday."

"I heard about the fire," said Bambi. "That explains why I can't call the truant officer. It doesn't answer my question." She pointed at Richard. "And who's your boyfriend?"

"Mr. B promised to show me blueprints for the new building. I came to see them," I chattered. "And he isn't my boyfriend. He's my friend, Richard Park."

"There are no blueprints here, young lady. And there's not going to be any new building if I have anything to do with it." Then she took a deep breath, and her tone of voice changed abruptly. "But I'm glad you stopped in. I want to thank you. Tiffany told me you've agreed to talk to your grandmother about signing those papers allowing us to buy back her share of the restaurant."

"Tiffany lied. I didn't say that. Gramma Rosa won't sign away her share of the restaurant," I said.

"But if she got her money back, maybe she could help you go to college."

"I'm going to be a chef," I pointed out. "I'm going to culinary school. Maybe in Paris."

"Whatever. Explain to your grandmother that after she signs those papers she won't have responsibility for the restaurant. At her age, she needs her money to be in a nice, secure place. A place she doesn't have to worry about. Something could happen here at Baldacci's and all her money would be gone. My husband and I've never run a restaurant before. We haven't got the years of experience my father-in-law had."

I nodded. She was right about that.

"And did Tiffany tell you we might find a little role for you, should the television program happen?"

"She mentioned that."

Richard stared at me, "She promised you a part in the television show?"

"She was trying to bribe me."

"Cool!" said Richard.

"That show is very hush-hush," said Mrs. Baldacci. "Nothing definite. Nothing *can* be definite until we have your grandmother's signature. That's why it's so important she sign those papers as soon as possible." She paused. "Did you talk to her last night?"

"No," I answered, truthfully.

"Mikki, your future could depend on it. Money for your education, and a possible television role … why, you'd be the envy of all your friends. Wouldn't she, what was your name?"

"Richard," said Richard.

"Richard, of course. Such a manly name."

Richard looked as though he was ready to throw up.

"You'll go home and talk with your grandmother now, won't you?" Bambi persisted.

"My grandmother isn't *at* home right now," I said. "She's in the hospital. Last night someone broke into our house and poisoned her."

"What?" Bambi seemed stricken. "How could that happen?"

"I don't know. But the police are investigating," I assured her.

"Bambi! Bambi! I need you! Upstairs!" Tiffany's voice was shrill and frantic and loud enough to be heard even over the electric drill pulsating somewhere in the building.

Bambi Baldacci turned and ran up the stairs to the restaurant.

Richard and I followed her.

Chapter 40

The restaurant was even busier that it had been the day before. Four women were pasting red velvet wallpaper on the walls of the ladies' room (purple velvet on the men's). They'd left the doors to both open so they could get their ladders and buckets in and out of the small rooms more easily.

The drills we'd heard were the electricians'. They'd finished putting ceiling fans up over the bar in the lounge and were now installing them in the restaurant.

The painters had finished the dining room.

The paintings of Italy were back on the walls.

I was so amazed by the changes made since yesterday that at first I didn't focus on the problem.

The problem was Angelo. He and Tito were in the lounge, and Angelo was furious. "How can you do this to Tony's memory?" Angelo said. "This … desecration!" He pulled one of the framed photographs from the wall, threw it on the floor, and stomped on it.

Seven or eight spaces on the wall were already empty. Angelo was working his way around the room.

"You hang pictures of the enemies of Tony's friends on the wall of his restaurant?" Crash! Another smashed picture hit the dust. "I spit on these people." He did. Angelo was a master spitter.

"You're destroying private property!" Tiffany screamed. "Bambi! Stop him! It took weeks to find all those pictures! Someone call the police!"

Tito stood by, grinning, but not participating in the carnage. He waved at me. I waved back.

"You know those guys?" Richard whispered.

"Sure. They're the ones who kidnapped me," I whispered back.

"Oh. Right," Richard answered. "What's the big crazy one doing?"

"Bambi and Tiffany must have hung pictures of families that competed with the D'Andreas. Angelo and Tito are very loyal," I replied.

"Bambi, see what he's doing? Stop him!" Tiffany stamped her foot. She looked as though she was about to cry. The wallpaper hangers and electricians had stopped working and were watching the show.

Bambi walked up to Angelo and grabbed his arm. "Stop it! Stop it, I said! This is not Tony's restaurant anymore! He's gone! I'll call the cops if you throw one more picture on the ground!"

Angelo glanced down at her and laughed. He brushed her hand off his arm as though she was an annoying fly. "Go ahead. Call the cops. You do that, and I'll tell them what your dear friend Tiffany was doing last night."

He grabbed another picture from the wall and spit directly on it. Splat! Then he threw it on top of the others on the newly black and white floor. "Morelli family pictures! In Baldacci's restaurant!"

Bambi turned to Tiffany. "What's he talking about? What were you doing last night?"

All of a sudden I got it. Tiffany was the one who'd poisoned Gramma Rosa!

I took off, dodging ladders and paint cans. Next thing I knew I was in the bar, lunging at her.

Angelo stepped back, out of my way.

I punched her - hard – with my right fist, right between those tattooed boobs, and grabbed at her hair with my left. We both went crashing down among the half-full paint cans stacked in the corner of the bar.

Tiffany's blonde hair ended up in my hand.

Who knew? Tiffany was a brunette.

Her wig dripped white paint.

When Angelo stopped laughing he bent down to boost me to my feet. He took the wig out of my hand and gently put her dripping hair back on Tiffany's head.

Her new look – blonde with white paint streaks - was distinctive.

Tiffany screamed and reached up to straighten her wig, white paint and blue mascara running down her cheeks. The crowd of assorted onlookers started applauding.

Richard cheered, "Yay, Mikki!"

At that moment Chief Hunter and Detective Adler walked in the front door.

Everyone fell silent.

"Good morning, everyone," he said. He checked out Tiffany, who was still sitting on the ground. "Looks as though we've arrived at an interesting moment."

"Nothing's going on!" Tiffany shut her mouth and carefully stood up, glaring at me and Angelo. She could have been a fire-breathing dragon just waiting to unleash her flames. A fire-breathing dragon wearing a crooked blonde wig half covered with dripping white paint.

"Would you by chance be Tiffany Schuman?" asked Chief Hunter, who was trying very hard not to smile.

"Yeah," said Tiffany. "You got a problem with that?"

"No problem at all. It means I have the duty to inform you that you are under arrest for the attempted murder of Mrs. Rosa

D'Andrea. You have the right to remain silent. Anything you say can and will be used against you in a court of law. You have the right to a lawyer. If you cannot afford a lawyer one will be appointed for you. Do you understand these rights?"

"Sure. I'm not stupid."

"What's happening?" asked Bambi, coming out of the corner she'd retreated to during the confusion. "I'm this young woman's employer. I demand to know what this is all about."

"Last night your employee broke into Mrs. Rosa D'Andrea's home and held a rag soaked in turpentine over her nose and mouth. Ms. Schuman may have believed Mrs. D'Andrea was dead, but she was only unconscious. This morning she was able to identify Ms. Schuman as her attacker."

"We saw her," Angelo spoke up. "Me and Tito can testify she went inside Mrs. D'Andrea's home about 7:10 last night. We didn't know she'd done that rag stuff, though. That was nasty!"

Tito nodded. "Yeah. We was there."

Chief Hunter frowned. "You were there? I thought only Mrs. D'Andrea's daughter and granddaughter were in the house."

"We wasn't in the house. We was across the street from the house. Keeping an eye on it, you know," said Angelo.

"To protect them," said Tito.

"Like bodyguards," said Angelo.

Richard had come over to stand next to me. "Great job they did," he whispered.

I concentrated on what was happening.

"I can tell the police something about you bozos, too!" said Tiffany, turning toward them. "It was you who started the fire that practically burned the town down yesterday!" She turned toward Chief Hunter. "Ask those inspectors who're checking for arson. These idiots set a time bomb under Robert Morelli's car. It was supposed to go off at seven o'clock in the morning, but they messed it up so it didn't go off until eight o'clock. Maybe there'll be part of it left in the wreckage!"

Tito and Angelo nudged each other and shrugged.

Chief Hunter looked at them, and then at Tiffany. "That's interesting information, Ms. Schuman. You're absolutely right. I understand a bomb was found in the wreckage. Except it didn't go off. Not at seven o'clock and not at eight o'clock. In fact, it didn't go off at all."

Angelo gave Tito a shove. "You idiot. You never get anything right."

"Which is not to say that attempting to make a bomb and attaching it to someone's car is not against the law." Chief Hunter didn't look happy.

"But then what started the fire?" I asked. "*Something* happened."

"Most definitely, something happened," said the chief. "There was another incendiary device attached to Mr. Morelli's car. That device was on a remote control that was activated at eight o'clock. That second device caused the explosion that started the fire."

Angelo frowned. "There wasn't no other bombs on the car when I put mine on it the night before. I would've noticed."

Chief Hunter nodded. "No doubt. The way the person who put their device on the car knew your bomb was there, and what it was set to, and knew if it didn't work, they could activate the back-up device and make you think you'd set the fire."

Angelo nodded. "That's what we thought, Chief. For sure."

"The only person who would have known that was the person who put the second bomb there." Chief Hunter looked at Tiffany.

"Why're you staring at me?" said Tiffany. "How would I know anything about bombs? And why would I want to blow up some teacher's car?"

"I haven't figured that out yet," admitted Chief Hunter.

"I have," I said, raising my hand as though I was in school. Blood dripped onto the floor. It was oozing from a dozen cuts on both my hands. I must have landed on some of the broken glass from the picture frames when Tiffany and I fell into the paint cans.

But this was no time to worry about a little blood.

Chief Hunter looked at me. "You have something to add, Mikki?"

"Tiffany wanted to be a television star. She and Bambi Baldacci planned to produce a reality television show here, in this restaurant, about gangsters and their families. Bambi asked Mr. Baldacci to give Tiffany a job as hostess here. But Tiffany's real job was to take pictures of the customers, and learn what Edgewood was like, now, and in the past. She and Bambi tried to convince Mr. Baldacci to let them use the restaurant for the television show. He refused. Then he announced that he and my grandmother were going to renovate the restaurant. It wouldn't look the same; it would be modern. Tiffany and Bambi would lose all the work they'd done to create a show around an old Italian restaurant."

Everyone was listening to me. This was no time to get nervous.

"Tiffany thought if Mr. Baldacci were dead, Bambi and her husband would inherit the restaurant, and they could still make the TV show. So she came to the restaurant early the morning after Mr. Baldacci announced the renovations. Maybe she said she was here to congratulate him. She slipped cyanide into his cup of coffee and then took her own cup upstairs to the bar to wash it out so no one would know someone else had been in his office."

"Wait a minute, Mikki," said Chief Hunter. "That's an imaginative story, but where would a young woman like Tiffany get cyanide?"

"She made it," I said. "Or maybe she stole it from one of the pharmaceutical companies where she worked summer internships while she was in college. Tiffany looks a lot dumber than she is. She has a degree in chemistry. Okay if I go on, Chief?"

"Go right ahead," he said, grinning.

"So Tiffany was gone before the EMTs got here. When Richard and I came in the service entrance downstairs we heard the crash in the bar, but didn't go upstairs. We tried to revive Mr. Baldacci and we called 911. She had plenty of time to leave."

"But what about Mrs. D'Andrea? And this bomb thing?" asked Chief Hunter.

"At first no one questioned that Mr. Baldacci's death was natural. But then, people," Chief Hunter was smiling quizzically. "Okay. Richard and I began asking questions. We told you, Chief Hunter, and I told Tito and Angelo. The guys thought maybe the Morelli crime family was active again." I looked at Angelo and Tito. "They decided to follow Robert Morelli, who teaches at the high school. They didn't find anything, but they got the idea to kill him, or at least scare him, to warn the Morelli family. Somehow Tiffany must have found out Angelo and Tito were looking for a murderer, and discovered the bomb they set under Mr. Morelli's car."

"We was talking about it when we was here the other day," said Tito. "Remember, Angelo? When that Tiffany babe threw us out."

"That ditzy dame must of heard us," said Tito, hitting Angelo's shoulder. "I told you to shut up about it."

Angelo shrugged.

I grinned. "So Tiffany figured if either Angelo and Tito or the Morellis were framed for Mr. B's death that would take attention away from her. She could tell the police it was them, and they'd be arrested. Case closed. But she had to be sure her plan was perfect. She checked their bomb, and realized it might not go off. That would ruin everything. So she made one of her own and put it under Mr. Morelli's car, too, as insurance. From what you said, I guess it was her bomb that went off, not theirs."

"And your grandmother?" asked Chief Hunter.

"She was a silent partner in the restaurant. After Mr. Baldacci died, Bambi and her husband wanted Gramma Rosa to sell her part to them. Gramma refused. Yesterday afternoon Tiffany offered me a role in the TV show if I'd convince my grandmother to sign and take the buy-out. I wouldn't do it. Tiffany must have been so frantic about the television show she decided to kill Gramma Rosa, too. Maybe she figured my mom, who'd inherit from Gramma, would be easier to deal with."

I took a deep breath.

"Is that all, Mikki?" said Chief Hunter.

"I think so. Sir." I said.

Baldacci's restaurant was very quiet.

"I want a lawyer," said Tiffany.

"That's a good idea," said Chief Hunter. "Tito, Angelo, you boys better come down to the station with me, too. Putting bombs under cars, even if they don't go off, isn't neighborly."

As Detective Adler took Tiffany and the men outside, Chief Hunter turned to me. "Your mother never called me," he said.

"She's been busy," I answered. "I'll give her your message when I get home. Promise."

"I may need to go over some of those details later," he added. "Maybe we could all get together."

"We have to get Gramma Rosa home and feeling better," I reminded him.

He nodded. "Your family has had a rough week." He looked over at Richard. "I'm glad you have a friend in Edgewood. I hope you know police can be your friends, too."

Chapter 41

Mom left before Dad rang the doorbell Friday night. She had her own dinner date. How was I supposed to know she and Chief Hunter had gone to the senior prom together back in the dark ages?

"Dad, this is Gramma Rosa," I said. He looked nervous. I was nervous myself.

I was still angry with him for leaving Mom and me. I wasn't ready to have a long talk with him. At least we were meeting Sung Ja and her mom in the restaurant.

What do you say to your best friend who is now living with your father? Was she going to be my stepsister some day? At least with all of us together we could be polite (even if it was hard.) Sung Ja and I had been best friends for years. I really did want to see her.

With the help of the new clothes Mom'd bought me, I felt pretty good, despite my bruises. And the fact that I was tottering a bit on my high boots. "I need to get my jacket," I told Dad. I wanted to check the mirror one more time.

I left Dad and Gramma Rosa in the living room making polite conversation while I went back to my room. My mirror showed I didn't look bad. None of my bruises showed.

I wanted to prove to Dad that I'd grown up. Mom and I were doing just fine without him.

I did a quick turn to check the back of my jacket.

I turned, but my ankle in its high boot didn't. I grabbed the bookcase, thinking it would keep me from falling.

Instead, the shelves fell with me, sending me, and my books, colliding onto the floor of my room. I wasn't hurt. Just mortified. This was definitely not the way I'd planned the evening to begin. Books and I had not had a good week.

I looked up from my bedroom floor to see Dad standing in the doorway. "Are you all right? Your grandmother and I heard a crash."

"I'm fine." I crawled out from under the bookcase, got back on my feet, dusted myself off and checked to make sure my boots were all right. "I just slipped a little."

I waited for Dad to make one of his "You're such a klutz" remarks.

All he said was, "Nice boots."

Then I waited for him to say how I was too young to wear them, or how he'd have to pay for the medical bills, or why didn't I change into a more sensible pair of shoes. Instead, he reached down and picked up Cat, who'd been pushed off the bed when the bookcase fell. He paused, and then put her back on my bed. Then he picked up Saint Lawrence. "Who's this?"

"Saint Lawrence, the patron saint of chefs. Mr. Baldacci, a friend of Gramma Rosa's and mine, gave him to me," I explained.

"I'm afraid Saint Lawrence got a little damaged," Dad said, handing him back to me. "His base seems to have come loose."

I sat down on the bed, books at my feet, and examined at the statue. My eyes started to fill. Not after everything that had happened this week. How could I have broken Mr. B's special Saint Lawrence statue?

There was definitely a crack in the base.

Then I looked closer.

"I think maybe it's supposed to open," I said. "Look," I showed Dad. "Maybe the bottom screws off."

"Try it," he said. "Maybe there's a hidden treasure in there."

I shook it. "I don't think so," I said. But, very carefully, I started to turn the base. And it started moving. Slowly, but surely. And then a little faster. "It's definitely coming off!"

Inside was a piece of paper, folded small.

I looked up at Dad.

"Go ahead. Open it," he said.

"I think Gramma Rosa should be here when I do," I said. "Mr. B was her friend first."

I picked up Saint Lawrence and the base, and the paper, and went to the living room and showed Gramma Rosa what I'd found.

She was as excited as I was. "I don't know anything about it, Mikki. But Tony gave the statue to you, so it's you who must read what is on the paper."

Very carefully, I opened it.

But I'm not going to tell you what was written there.

Because it's a secret.

The ultra-secret family recipe for Mr. B's special tomato sauce, that he would never give to anyone outside his family.

He gave it to me.

The note said he thought of me as family. That he hoped someday I could use the recipe in my own restaurant.

I started to cry.

Sometimes being happy is a good reason to cry.

I even let Dad hug me. A little. He'll never really understand what happened to Mom and Gramma Rosa and me in the past week. But he says he'll try. He doesn't need to understand everything. He has a new life now, and so do we.

Even Sung Ja's changed. She's gotten three piercings in her left ear and become a vegetarian. We need to talk about that.

And maybe the tomato sauce will be used again at Baldacci's.

Gramma Rosa says she's going to buy Bambi and Luc out, and find a new chef. At least until I'm old enough to inherit the restaurant.

I don't know how it'll all work out. But I do know I'll always cherish Saint Lawrence, and what Mr. B left me.

And my family. All of it.

##

RECIPES FROM MIKKI'S COOKBOOK

MIKKI'S MARVELOUS MAC & CHEESE

1 box (1 pound) whole wheat dry macaroni
Salt
A little butter or olive oil
Black pepper
Cayenne
Dry mustard
Approximately 1 ½ cups milk
4 cups of grated hard cheese. Use at least 2 of your favorite varieties, preferably more.
Include extra sharp cheddar and Swiss. Other kinds that add awesome flavor are Asiago, Parmesan, Gruyere, and Jarlsberg. (Save your blue cheeses for other recipes.)

Heat oven to 350 degrees.

Heat water and a tablespoonful of oil in a large pan. (The oil keeps the macaroni from sticking.) When water boils, add pasta and cook until "al dente," or for the shortest time suggested on the package. Remove from heat and strain.

While water is heating and pasta is cooking, grate and mix cheeses.

Rub the oil or butter lightly on the inside of the casserole dish. Add 1/3 of cooked pasta. Then add 1/3 of the cheeses. Sprinkle with salt,

¼ teaspoon pepper, ¼ teaspoon cayenne, 1 teaspoon dry mustard. Then add another third of the pasta and repeat. Finally, the rest of the pasta, the last of the cheeses, and the spices.

Pour in just enough milk so it reaches the top layer of pasta.

Put casserole dish in oven and cook until it is bubbly and browned on top – approximately 45 minutes.

Will serve 4-6 people.
Served with a salad or a green leafy vegetable like spinach, kale, mustard or collard greens. It's even better re-heated the next day, so making it ahead is a great idea.

WILD BLUEBERRY PANCAKES

1 egg
1 ½ cups wild blueberries (cleaned, if fresh; drained, if frozen)
1 cup flour
2 Tablespoons sugar
1 Tablespoon maple syrup
2 teaspoons baking powder
½ teaspoon salt
3 Tablespoons melted butter
1 cup milk
1 Tablespoon lemon juice

Separate egg yolk and white. Beat egg white until it is stiff.
Mix egg yolk, milk, lemon juice, maple syrup and melted butter together.
Blend flour, sugar, baking powder and salt.
Mix dry ingredients and liquids.
Stir until all the flour is moist. (The batter will be slightly lumpy. That's okay.)
Stir in the blueberries.
Finally, stir in the egg white.

Lightly oil griddle or frying pan. (If it is a "non-stick" pan, oil is not necessary.)
Heat until drops of water sizzle when dropped onto cooking surface.

Drop batter onto griddle using large spoon.
Turn pancakes when they are puffed and full of bubbles.
Brown on both sides.

Serve with butter and warm maple syrup.

Makes 14-16 four inch pancakes.

ONION POPOVERS

2 eggs (room temperature)
1 cup milk (room temperature)
1 cup flour
¾ teaspoon salt
1/2 cup onion, sliced & diced into small, thin pieces
A little butter or olive oil

Pre-heat oven to 430 degrees.

Popovers may be cooked in popover pan or large 6-cupcake pan. (If you cook the batter in a casserole or baking dish it's called Yorkshire Pudding.) Oil or butter the bottom of your pans lightly.

Beat eggs for about a minute. Add milk and beat until blended. Add onions and beat briefly.

Mix flour and salt. Add egg mixture. Stir until flour is moist. Beat about a minute.

Pour batter about 1/3-1/2 way up in pans. Bake 35 minutes. Turn oven down to 375; continue baking another 15 minutes.

Serve hot.
Makes 6 large popovers.

YUMMY CINNAMON BREAD

¼ pound salted butter, melted (1 stick)
2 cups flour
3 teaspoons baking powder
2 eggs
1 1/2 cups sugar
¾ cup milk
4 Tablespoons cinnamon
½ teaspoon salt

Pre-heat oven to 360 degrees. Butter loaf pan (8 ½" x 4 ½" x 3").

Mix flour, baking powder, 2 Tablespoons cinnamon and salt. Beat eggs until thick. Slowly beat in 1 cup sugar. Add ¼ cup of melted butter (not all of butter.) Beat slightly.

Add dry ingredients, alternating with milk. Blend.

Pour batter into loaf pan.

Mix ½ cup sugar and 2 Tablespoons cinnamon. Sprinkle over batter in loaf pan. Pour rest of melted butter over the top.

Using a knife, cut through the topping and the batter in loaf pan several times.

Bake 60 minutes.

Remove from oven. Let stand about 10 minutes, then remove from pan and cool on rack.

Makes 1 loaf. Great for breakfast or an afternoon snack.

Freezes well.

FRIED SQUASH

2-3 medium-sized summer (yellow) squash or zucchini
5-6 oz. crackers (plain, stoned wheat, or rice. NOT graham or crackers that
have flavors like barbecue, sour cream, etc.) or Panko flakes
vegetable or olive oil for frying
2-3 eggs

Beat eggs in shallow bowl.

Put crackers in closed plastic bag or between 2 pieces of waxed paper and break into crumbs by repeatedly rolling a rolling pin or glass over them. If you use Panko, crushing is not necessary. Put crumbs or Panko in another shallow bowl.

Wash summer squash or zucchini, dry, and slice in pieces a little less than ½ inch thick.

Cover bottom of large frying pan with olive or other oil. (Have cover for frying pan available. If your frying pan does not have a cover, use a cookie sheet to cover it.) Heat oil to medium high.

Dip pieces of squash first in beaten eggs, both sides, then in cracker crumbs, both sides, then place in frying pan. Repeat, until frying pan is full. (One layer.)

Turn after 5-7 minutes. Brown on second side for 3-4 minutes.

Cover pan and cook an additional 3 minutes to make sure squash pieces are cooked through. When they are done they should be brown on both sides and soft in the middle.

Remove pieces of fried squash and put on paper towels to absorb a little of the oil. Add a little oil to the pan and repeat until all squash is fried.

Serve hot.

MINIATURE CREAM PUFFS

Cream Puffs:

½ cup salted butter (1 stick)
1 cup water
1 cup flour
½ teaspoon salt
4 eggs
Confectioners' sugar or chocolate sauce

Heat oven to 400 degrees.

Mix butter and water in saucepan and heat to rolling boil, stirring.
Add flour and salt.
Reduce heat. Stir mixture at low heat until it forms a ball. This should take about 1 minute.
Take off heat.
Beat in eggs, one at a time, until mixture is smooth and a little shiny.
Using a teaspoon (or your clean hands) form batter into balls about the size of a large walnut and put them on an ungreased baking sheet. Remember to make the balls large enough so you can fill them after they are cooked, and leave space between them on the baking sheet.

Bake for 30 minutes, until the balls are puffed and dry.

When they're cool, cut off the tops with a sharp knife, scoop out the soft inside, and fill with one of the fillings listed below. Replace top. Sprinkle with confectioners' sugar or drip a little chocolate sauce on the top.

Makes 35-40

Fillings for Miniature Cream Puffs:

Your choice!

If you choose to fill your cream puffs with flavored whipped creams, be sure to whip your own cream; don't use pre-whipped mixtures. Experiment adding some of your favorite flavors to the cream as you whip it. Some of Mikki's favorites are

1. Cream whipped with vanilla and fine sugar. (Vanilla flavored whipped cream.)
2. Cream whipped with seedless raspberry jelly. (Raspberry flavored whipped cream.)
3. Cream whipped with cocoa powder – not instant cocoa – and fine sugar. (Chocolate flavored whipped cream.)

You may also fill the cream puffs with softened ice cream or pudding. Serve at once, or refrigerate. Put in freezer if you're filling with ice cream!

USA Today best-selling author Lea Wait grew up in the New Jersey suburbs, and, with time off for college and work in New York City, raised her own daughters there. She now lives on the coast of Maine. For more information about her and her books, see her website, http://www.leawait.com, friend her on Goodreads and Facebook, and sign up for her mailing list at leawait@roadrunner.com And if you enjoyed *Pizza To Die F*or, she'd love you to tell your friends, and post a review online.

OTHER BOOKS BY LEA WAIT

Historical Novels for ages 8 and up

Stopping to Home

Seaward Born

Wintering Well

Finest Kind

Uncertain Glory

Shadows Antique Print Mystery Series

Shadows at the Fair

Shadows on the Coast of Maine

Shadows on the Ivy

Shadows at the Spring Show

Shadows of a Down East Summer

Shadows on a Cape Cod Wedding

Shadows on a Maine Christmas

Shadows on a Morning in Maine

Mainely Needlepoint Mystery Series

Twisted Threads

Threads of Evidence

Thread and Gone

Dangling By a Thread

Tightening the Threads

Thread the Halls

Thread Herrings

Maine Café Mystery Series (under name Cornelia Kidd)

Kindred Spirits

Nonfiction

Living and Writing on the Coast of Maine

CPSIA information can be obtained
at www.ICGtesting.com
Printed in the USA
LVOW10s0219161117
556510LV00018B/813/P